W9-ANQ-564

TO THE FRONTIER

THE ADVENTURES OF YOUNG BUFFALO BILL

TO THE FRONTIER

E. CODY KIMMEL

ILLUSTRATED BY SCOTT SNOW

HARPERCOLLINS*PUBLISHERS*

**Grateful acknowledgments and thanks to
Mark Bureman of the Leavenworth County Historical Society
and to the following people and organizations:**

Betty and Paul Strand and the Leavenworth County Historical Society,
Leavenworth, Kansas;
Etta Brill and the Weston Historical Museum, Weston, Missouri;
Otto Ewoldt and the Buffalo Bill Museum of LeClaire, Iowa;
Matt Shaffer and the State Historical Society of Iowa, Iowa City, Iowa;
The Davenport Library Special Collection, Davenport, Iowa;
The Shaffer Law Office, Weston, Missouri;
Sandy Reed, Larry DePover, and the Cody Homestead, Princeton, Iowa;
Kansas State Historical Society, Topeka, Kansas;
Stephen Allie and the Frontier Army Museum,
Fort Leavenworth, Kansas;
And most special thanks and general adoration for
Marcia Wernick and Alix Reid.

 Printed in the United States of America. For information address HarperCollins Children's Books, a division of HarperCollins Publishers, 1350 Avenue of the Americas, New York, NY 10019.
www.harperchildrens.com

Library of Congress Cataloging-in-Publication Data
Kimmel, E. Cody.
To the Frontier / E. Cody Kimmel ; illustrated by Scott Snow.
p. cm. — (The boyhood adventures of Buffalo Bill Cody)
Summary: After the death of his brother, eight-year-old Bill Cody and his family set out from Iowa to make a new home for themselves in the volatile Kansas Territory.
ISBN 0-06-029117-6 — ISBN 0-06-029118-4 (lib. bdg.)
1. Buffalo Bill, 1846–1917—Childhood and youth—Juvenile fiction. [1. Buffalo Bill, 1846–1917—Childhood and youth—Fiction. 2. Frontier and pioneer life—Kansas—Fiction. 3. Kansas—History—1854–1861—Fiction.] I. Snow, Scott, ill. II. Title.
PZ7.K56475 To 2002 00-063170
[Fic]—dc21 CIP
AC

Typography by Andrea Vandergrift
1 3 5 7 9 10 8 6 4 2
❖
First Edition

★ ★ ★ ★ ★

For my remarkable dad,
William Frederic Cody, who
first told me about Buffalo Bill
—E.C.K.

★ ★ ★ ★ ★

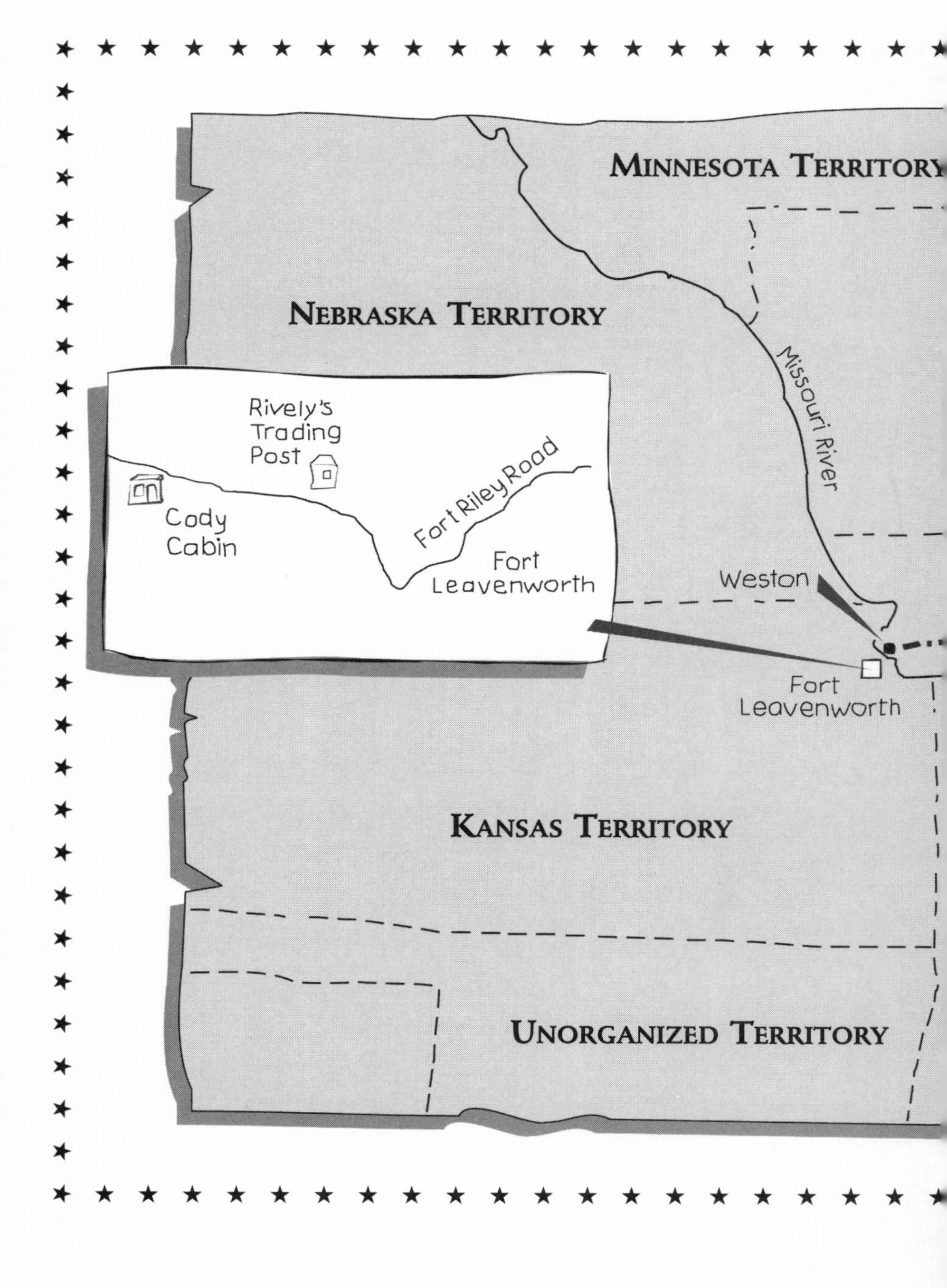
Minnesota Territory
Nebraska Territory
Missouri River
Rively's Trading Post
Cody Cabin
Fort Riley Road
Fort Leavenworth
Weston
Fort Leavenworth
Kansas Territory
Unorganized Territory

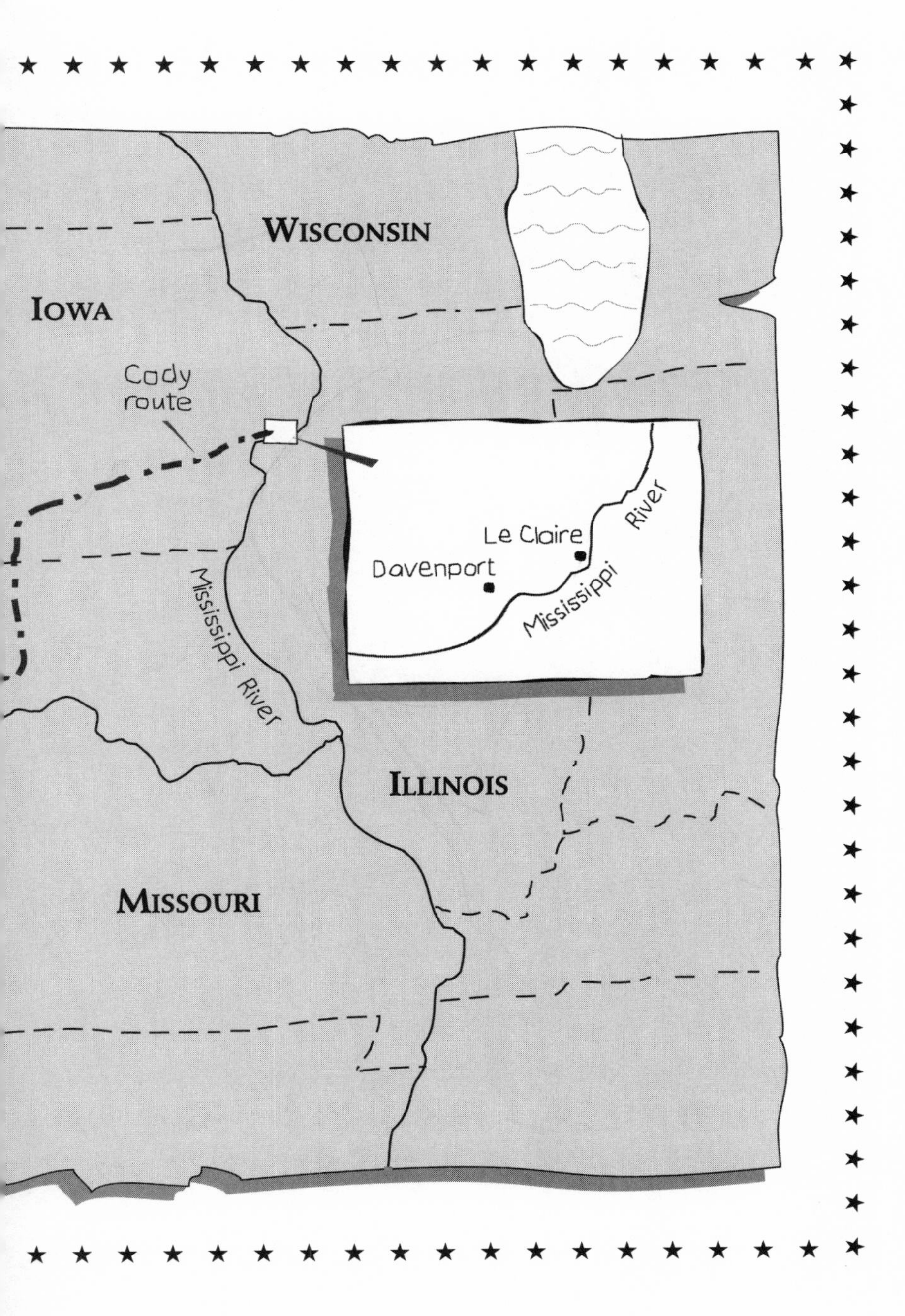

WISCONSIN
IOWA
Cody route
Le Claire
Davenport
Mississippi River
Mississippi River
ILLINOIS
MISSOURI

CONTENTS

★ ★ ★ ★ ★

Chapter One

LECLAIRE, IOWA

★ ★ ★

Nothing would ever be the same.

From high in the branches of the old elm folks called the Green Tree Hotel, Bill Cody looked down at the great river just a stone's throw away. In the morning he would be leaving Iowa, the only home he had ever known. The Mississippi River had been his companion and teacher for as long as he could remember. He had learned most every thing he knew about the world here in the branches of the Green

Tree, watching the steamboats go by and listening to the stories of the river pilots strolling below—stories of the lands they had seen on their travels, of thriving towns, pioneers, and Indians.

There was a time Bill would have given anything to leave LeClaire and travel west to see some of those sights himself. But now that his family was preparing to do just that, packing all their belongings into two prairie schooners to begin a new life, Bill didn't feel excited, or even happy. He had barely been able to feel anything since his brother, Sammy, had died.

Ma had told Sammy a hundred times not to ride that horse. Bill himself had sensed Betsy was overly spooky and skittish that day, and thought about telling Sammy so, but what twelve-year-old boy ever took advice from a brother four years younger? So Bill kept silent, and Sammy climbed onto Betsy's back. When she reared up, Sammy held on tight, laughing when she failed to throw him. But then she reared again, so wildly she landed right on her back, Sammy still in the saddle. And there was no doctor, in LeClaire or anywhere, upriver or down, who could save Sammy then.

Pa talked about the opportunities that awaited them in the West. How it wouldn't be long before the government passed a law allowing families to settle in the Kansas and Nebraska territories, across the Missouri River. How they would have their pick of the good, rich land and be able to stake a claim and build a new house from the foundation up. But what Pa didn't talk about, what no one talked about, was the real reason for the move. That whatever waited for them in the new territories, there would be none of the constant reminders of Sammy that were everywhere here in Iowa. That was a lure more powerful than any promise of a new life.

"Anybody home?" a voice called from below. Bill's enormous mastiff hound, Turk, gave a welcoming bark from his position at the foot of the tree.

Bill didn't have to look down through the branches to know it was his friend Joe Barnes. They had grown up together and often spent time in the Green Tree Hotel. Bill watched Joe scramble expertly up the tree, and he made room on the wide branch. They sat in silence for a time.

"The *Kate Kearney* went down," Joe finally said, his gazed fixed somewhere on the Illinois bank of the river.

"She get herself snagged?" asked Bill about the steamer.

"Boiler blew," said Joe. "She went up in flames in seconds, the captains are saying. Over on the Missouri River." Joe paused. "Guess you'll be there yourself before long."

Bill nodded. He and Joe had made plans, pretty much as soon as they had learned how to talk, to become river pilots together. A boy growing up on the banks of the river called the Father of Waters couldn't want for a better job. River pilots did the most glamorous and dangerous work anywhere. Some of the best river pilots in the country lived right in LeClaire, their huge houses towering over Main Street, reminding everyone in town of their importance.

Bill and Joe had intended to apprentice themselves as soon as they were thirteen or fourteen. It would be hard work; it would take years to learn the trade—to memorize every inch of water, every bend, every tree and woodpile clear down to New Orleans. But like the river channels themselves, plans had a way of changing.

"I guess there's no chance . . ." Joe's voice trailed off.

"Nope," Bill replied. "The house is sold, and the papers signed. As long as the sun rises, we're leaving tomorrow. For good."

There was nothing that really needed saying, so Joe simply nodded. The sunlight on the river was growing soft and orange. Bill's stomach gave a rumble.

"Guess I better be getting on home then," Bill said.

"Guess you'd better," Joe said. Bill swung down onto a lower branch and dropped to the ground. Turk leaped to his feet and gave Bill's hand a warm lick.

"Hey, Bill?" Joe's voice called from the branches.

Bill looked up.

"See ya round," Joe said.

"See ya," Bill replied. Then, turning his back on his friend and their river, he and Turk began to walk home.

Truth was, Bill had never really thought about LeClaire until now. It had been home most of the time, except for the year they'd lived in the big stone house upriver while Pa cleared land for Mr. Brackenridge. But Bill had only been three, and didn't remember much of it.

As he walked up Main Street in the shadow of the grain and lumber mills, Bill tried to draw a picture of LeClaire in his mind—something to take with him when he left. The barrels and brooms lined up just so outside the dry-goods store. The hot smells and sharp sounds of the blacksmith shop. The candy store and bakery. The streams of visitors passing through the great front door of the Hotel Berlin.

Some distance away there was someone sitting over on the big boulder Bill sometimes pretended was his stagecoach. Stepping off Main Street and walking closer, he saw it was his older sister Julia. She looked lost in thought, but her face quickly broke into a smile at the sight of him.

"Care to take the reins?" she asked, holding the imaginary leather straps out.

He sat down next to her on the boulder where he'd spent hours with Julia, Sammy, and Joe playing Iowa's Fastest and Bravest Stagecoach Driver. It seemed silly now, just a day before they were to leave on a real trip in a real wagon, but Julia's brown eyes shone eagerly. And they'd never be able to play this game again, at least not on this particular rock. Bill gave the reins a little flick and felt himself falling into the game. Turk had seen this before and knew what was coming. With a little sigh, he turned in circles several times and curled up by the rock to wait.

"Stagecoach Bill, Iowa's fastest and bravest driver, urges his powerful team of horses on," Bill began.

"Who's along today?" Julia asked.

"Kit Carson," Bill said, glancing proudly at the famed scout and frontiersman now seated in the back of the deluxe Concord coach. Stagecoach Bill drove only the best, and this coach was built solidly of white oak and iron bands, its red-painted body adorned with sidelights and individual candle lamps for the travelers within. There was room for nine, so Bill added another passenger.

"And Colonel Kearney is along, too, on important business to Fort Leavenworth," Bill continued. "But my heavens! What's that behind us? Look at the size of it, Private Julia. Giddup, horses! Giddup!"

"What is it, Bill? What's after us?"

"A cyclone is all!" he shouted, cracking his imaginary whip with all his might. "Big as Davenport's gristmill, and twice as high! We'll have to outrun it. Hold on, folks. Fly, boys, fly!"

Julia tightened her grip on the rock as Bill cracked the whip again. She was a young lady now, eleven years old, and Bill knew that according to Ma, she was too old for these games. But Bill loved to have her along, especially with Sammy gone. She always made him feel that the game was as important to her as it was to him, and he worked hard to make her feel she was right there in the midst of danger. He could see he was doing a good job. The lurch of the stagecoach seemed so real, the roar of the cyclone so true, Julia had goose bumps on her arms.

Bill called out, "Hold on, Mr. Carson. Hold on, Colonel. If we cut up along the ridge, I think we can—" He broke off.

Julia looked up, wondering why her brother had stopped talking. She immediately saw the reason coming toward them with a purposeful stride. Martha. Their half sister and the oldest of the Cody children. Bill stared at her, his hands still raised and his fingers still tightly gripping the phantom reins.

"I have been looking all over town for the two of you," Martha scolded as soon as she was in earshot. "Have you both taken leave of your senses? The wagons are only half loaded, and there's so much to do. Ma's in a state, and here you are playing baby games! Bill, you know how Ma worries when you run off."

Bill knew all too well how Ma worried about him. He scowled slightly and looked at his feet.

Martha gave Julia a special disapproving look.

"And you, Julia. For shame. You're old enough to know better."

Bill was embarrassed for Julia, and Julia looked as if she was ready to give her older sister a piece of her mind. She opened her mouth, but Bill spoke first.

"Julia was just having a rest," he said, getting to his feet. "I'm the one who was playing."

"Well, you're both a sight," said Martha. "Come along home. It's like a circus—everything in crates and all of Pa's friends dropping by at once." She turned on her heel and started marching back home.

Julia and Bill exchanged a grin behind Martha's back as they followed their sister meekly up Main

Street, Turk trotting lightly behind.

As they approached their home, they could see Martha had barely exaggerated. Their two wagons and one carriage stood outside the plain two-story building. The wagons were sturdy prairie schooners made of oak wood, and each was covered with a large piece of well-oiled canvas that would protect their belongings from rain, dust, and sunlight. Those same belongings were piled everywhere in stacks on the ground. Each wagon was partially packed with more boxes and bags, some of which had tipped over or were even spilling out of the schooner's back end.

The horse-drawn carriage didn't have any boxes in it. This was where Ma and the girls would travel. It had been scrubbed and polished so that it gleamed like a diamond in the May sun. This carriage was Pa's pride and joy, purchased with profits he had earned driving the mail stagecoach from Davenport to Chicago for a whole year.

Pa would be driving one of the prairie schooners, and George Yancey, their hired man, the other. Both would be pulled by teams of oxen. Ma would drive the carriage. But Bill didn't plan to ride in either the wagons or the carriage. Pa had promised to make Bill an official scout on their journey. He would ride on horseback at the head of the procession, with Turk following behind. Like Kit Carson himself, he would seek out the dangers ahead with his keen young eyes, and he would keep his family safe from all harm. Nothing would frighten or threaten him, not stampeding buffalo, not hungry wolves, not venomous sharp-fanged snakes. . . .

"William Frederick Cody, are you listening to me?"

Bill startled upright, the wagons and crates all around him suddenly coming into focus.

"Yes, Ma. I mean, no, Ma. I'm sorry, I didn't hear," Bill said sheepishly, stepping back as George walked by loaded with several heavy boxes.

"You mean you weren't listening," Ma said. Her blue eyes, bright as a prairie sky, looked over him anxiously. "You didn't tell me you were running off, Bill. I was worried about you."

"I didn't run off, Ma," Bill said, trying his hardest not to sound as irritated as he felt. "I was just at the Green Tree with Joe. Saying good-bye and all. And Turk was with me the whole time."

Ma didn't look quite satisfied, but her worried expression softened at the sound of Joe's name.

"You'll miss him, won't you," she said with sympathy.

Something terrible, Bill thought. But he only nodded.

"I know it isn't easy," Ma said. "But I need to know where you are, Bill. Especially once we've gotten under way. No more running off. You must promise me that."

Ever since Sammy had died, Bill had felt there was a huge gaping hole in his ma where there used to be spirit and laughter. There was a hole in all of them, but especially in Ma. "I promise, Ma," Bill said, a little dully. Ma rewarded him with a small smile, a rare enough thing these days. She was beautiful, though her face looked tired in a way it hadn't six months before.

"I need you to nail down the lids on the kitchen crates and get them into the wagon if you can lift them yourself."

"Julia can help me," Bill said, looking around for his sister.

He regretted the suggestion as soon as he'd made it. Lifting crates was no job for a young lady, and he waited for Ma to say so, sorry that he'd started trouble. But Ma said nothing, only gave him a little look. Bill gave her a wide smile and started for the front door. Ma probably figured the taming of Julia would simply have to wait until they were settled once again, with a proper household around them.

The house was as messy inside as it was outside. As he passed more and more crates in the pantry and hallway, Bill couldn't believe the house was big enough to hold all the belongings they were now trying to pack. Bill came to the kitchen and saw the crates his mother had mentioned. Some of them were flipped upside down to serve as chairs for the men gathered there with Pa. Captain Davenport was there, and Mr. Goldsmith, the rapids pilot and stage-coach driver. Joe's pa, Mr. Barnes, was there, too, with Mr. Parkhurst, the general merchant. By the stove next to Pa stood Dr. Gamble, the kindly doctor who had ministered to Sammy in his final hours. Anyone who counted for anything in LeClaire was crowded into the room, and they all seemed to be talking at once.

"My brother Elijah's letter is very clear," Bill could hear Pa saying above the din. "The bill is certain to pass."

Mr. Goldsmith shook his head. "There have been meetings throughout the East, protesting this, Isaac. Strong resolutions against the repeal of the Missouri Compromise have been presented. How can you be so sure?"

Pa turned to Mr. Goldsmith. "Elijah's source is a congressman himself." The other men murmured. Pa continued. "I don't pretend to like it, Harvey. The government agreed fair and square that there would be no new slave states this far north, and now they're going back on it. But we're talking about prime land here, and any man can stake his claim. Elijah has business in the Kansas Territory, trading with the

Kickapoo. If he says the land is rich, then rich it is."

"It isn't as if they're outright allowing slavery," said Mr. Barnes. "As I hear it, they'll be putting the matter to a vote amongst the settlers."

"And a bloody business that will be," Captain Davenport interjected with feeling. "I spent enough years as sheriff of this town to know a thing or two about how men act when their own interests are at stake."

The men nodded gravely. No one noticed Bill, who was standing in the doorway holding a hammer of George's that he'd grabbed.

Bill had heard plenty of talk about this slavery question. Back when Pa was just a boy, the government had said that no new states north of a certain boundary would permit slavery. In exchange, the Union admitted Missouri as a slave state, and the whole thing was referred to as the Missouri Compromise. It was supposed to make everybody feel they'd gotten their own way. Southern states allowing slavery were satisfied that their new neighbors in Missouri would be slaveholders. Northern states that didn't allow slavery felt reassured that it was being limited to the South. But now there was talk of passing a bill to open up some of that new land to settlers, and letting those settlers decide the matter for themselves.

"But they're only trying to let the issue be fairly

decided," Mr. Parkhurst was protesting, lighting his pipe. "To let each man in these new territories have a say, based on his own interests and traditions. What could be more in keeping with the wishes of our Founding Fathers?"

"Surely the Founding Fathers did not foresee the continuing enslavement of man by man in their vision of our new world, Waldo," said the captain, a little sharply.

"Hear! Hear!" said Dr. Gamble in his gentle, scratchy voice. "This institution of slavery is nothing more than a withering curse on our lands. I'm not sure you fully understand, Isaac, what this conflict might mean to the territories, and to our country. If this issue is not resolved by our government, slavers could take up arms against Free-Soilers. There may be bloodshed, even civil war."

Pa looked thoughtful. "Well, Doc, I'm with you about slavery being a curse, and I would never own a slave myself. But I think there's plenty of folks just like me who ain't so riled up about it. Let them that's of a mind to go to meetings and shout at one another. I myself intend to stay well clear of it."

Bill decided he agreed with Pa. Slavery was wrong, but it just didn't have anything to do with the Codys. All they wanted was some decent land to farm, and a new life to live. How much could this question really matter to them? Bill shifted his weight from one foot to the other, and the hammer dropped to the floor with a *thud*. Suddenly all eyes in the room were on him, and the conversation stopped.

"Ma wants these crates on the wagon," Bill said, a little red-faced. "I reckon Julia can handle the little ones, but I best handle the bigger myself."

He bristled at the roar of laughter that broke out among the men. Were they laughing at the idea of Julia doing such work, or was it Bill himself they found so funny? Just because he wasn't grown up yet didn't mean he couldn't lift a crate. Either way, he was glad Julia was safely outside and unable to hear the chuckling.

"Julia will have her hands full enough tending Nellie and Mary Hannah, I expect," said Pa. "We'll give you a hand, Bill, if you don't mind."

Talk of politics gave way to joking and good-natured teasing as all the men pitched in to help. The heavy crates were nailed secure and loaded, one at a time, onto the wagons. The piles of boxes outside were organized and stowed away, and at last it seemed to Bill that they were more packed than not. The house was practically empty. Only the kitchen table and bedsteads remained. Pa would build new ones when they reached Kansas Territory.

The house grew quieter as Pa's friends left one by one. When the last of them had gone, and the spring evening was upon them, it was time to eat.

As the Codys gathered at the table, using empty crates for chairs, Bill looked around at the faces of his family. Martha fussed over Eliza Alice, correcting her posture and smoothing her hair. At six, Eliza Alice was old enough to be Martha's new project. Unlike Julia, she enjoyed the attention from her grown-up sister and was diligent in her attempts to act like a little lady. Across the table Julia shushed Nellie and bounced the baby, Mary Hannah, on her lap. She managed to watch over her sisters and look a thousand dreamy miles away at the same time. Five sisters, Bill thought. Sometimes it still amazed him.

Pa took his seat at the head of the table as Ma served up their last LeClaire supper, placing bread and cold slices of meat on odd bits of china too cracked or chipped to be worth packing. As Pa gave the blessing, Bill took his sisters' hands, Julia on one side of him and Eliza Alice on the other. There was warmth in their circle, but Bill remembered the feel of Sammy's hand in his own, and that absence the family no longer spoke of seemed overwhelming. Bill added a silent prayer to his father's blessing.

Keep us safe on our journey, Lord, and please . . . don't take any more of us.

Chapter Two

TAKING LEAVE

It was still dark, and quiet as the grave. Bill rose silently, crept down the stairs, and headed for the front door. There was something to be said for sleeping in your clothes—it made for a quick exit on rising. Turk rose from his sleeping area in the kitchen, stretched his massive legs, and followed Bill out the door.

There was no moon, and the sun had not yet pinked the sky. Bill didn't need light, though. His feet knew every bend of the path, every swell of Main Street, all the way to the riverfront. He could walk it blindfolded. In fact he had once, with Sammy, for a laugh.

His shoes were wet with dew by the time he

reached the Green Tree. He swung himself up easily. Turk, always impatient when Bill climbed somewhere he could not follow, gave a little whine and sat down. Bill could feel the river below, though he could not see it—a water-cooled breeze chilled his face, and the sound of soft ripples and waves teased his ears.

How many westwarders had Bill and Joe watched cross the Mississippi from this very place? They streamed across the river in herds, in wagons or on horseback, stopping in town just long enough to provision up before continuing in the direction of the setting sun. LeClaire was just an early chapter in their journeys, and the ends of their tales always remained unknown to Bill.

Now he was going to join their story. He turned from the river, facing northwest. Somewhere, miles through the dark, was Sammy's grave in the Long Grove Cemetery. Bill had spent countless hours sitting by the headstone there, telling Sammy every little thing that happened. Bill now made a promise to his brother. To return someday to Iowa and visit the grave. To bring honor to his brother's name with his own behavior. And above all, to remember. No matter what life brought him, no matter where it took him, he promised he would remember Sammy.

Bill jumped down onto the grass, now delicately

tinged with rosy light, and walked back home to his family. He was ready to go.

In spite of the early hour, it seemed half of LeClaire had turned out to bid the Codys farewell. Ma and Martha stood surrounded by friends, as Eliza Alice sat primly in the family carriage.

Bill felt almost sick with impatience as he paced back and forth between the prairie schooners. Both the wagons were packed. The teams were yoked. Pa was still inside, squaring away last-minute details with the new owner of the house. George, who would drive the heavier wagon, stood silently by the oxen awaiting instructions. Even Turk stood at attention. Bill had little use for these good-byes. He had already taken leave of all the neighbors he cared to.

Julia scrambled by, chasing Nellie. She paused long enough to exchange an exasperated look with her brother.

"Good-bye, good luck, godspeed—what more can there possibly be to go on about?" she said, and Bill grinned as she resumed her pursuit of Nellie.

The horse Bill would be riding, Orion, stood off to the side of the wagons. Bill wasn't old enough yet to have a horse of his own, and Orion was his favorite of all Pa's horses, the one he always chose to ride. Unable to stand still any longer, Bill walked over to Orion and swung himself up into the saddle. He whistled to Turk, who quickly trotted over.

Now here was a view. High in the saddle, in front of the wagons, Bill would see everything first when they were on the trail. He would be the real explorer. No matter that his father planned to follow the established stagecoach routes across Iowa, instead of breaking a new trail. No matter that his mother planned for them to spend their nights with friends or in respectable inns, rather than camping out. There still might be flooded rivers to ford, prairie fires to outrun, or even bandits to battle.

"Bill Cody, what in heaven are you doing?" his mother called, breaking away from a little group of neighbors and walking toward him.

"Just readying myself, Ma," he replied.

"You just ready yourself alongside your sisters in the carriage, Bill. Now get down off that horse before the crowd spooks him."

Bill felt a sudden sick feeling in his stomach at the thought of spending their voyage cooped up in the fancy rig.

"But Pa said . . ." he began quietly. It wasn't safe to push Ma these days, especially when horseback riding was involved. Bill knew that. But Pa had promised he could be the scout. Looking over the heads of the neighbors standing about, he caught his father's eye and sent him a look of appeal. Moments later, Pa stood by his stirrup.

"Isaac, tell the boy to get down," Ma said. "This is no day trip to McAusland. We are crossing two states."

"He'll come to no harm on Orion, Mary," Pa said gently.

"There could be mud holes. Or snakes."

"Turk will give warning," Pa countered, as Bill listened anxiously.

"He is eight years old!"

"And has been riding Orion over half that long," Pa said. "I'll be right behind him, Mary. If it gets rough, Bill will get into the carriage with you just as soon as I tell him to."

"Yes, Ma, as soon as Pa says," Bill said.

His parents exchanged a long look with each other.

"Mary," Pa said, softly. "Come now. We must let the boy live a little."

"I'm hoping he'll live *a lot,* Isaac," Ma retorted. Then she turned on her heel and walked away.

Bill swallowed guiltily. He had not meant to cause an argument between his parents. Perhaps he should have just obeyed Ma without question. But she never wanted him to do anything since Sammy had died. She didn't want him riding alone, didn't want him climbing trees or even going swimming unless Pa was along. The last thing Bill wanted was for Ma to be worrying over him, but if he stopped doing all the things that scared her, he might as well not get out of bed in the morning.

"It's all right, son," Pa said. "It's time we were on our way, don't you think?"

Bill nodded vigorously. Now more than ever he wanted to leave LeClaire. He thought to himself what he had never said aloud—that he was tired of paying for Sammy's accident with his own caution. He was tired of walking instead of riding, of getting home long before supper while his friends stayed out playing. Even when he'd had the grippe earlier in the month, Ma had acted like he was at death's door and kept him in the house for an entire week. She worried about him even when he was right in front of her, tucked into bed. Bill wondered if Ma would ever realize that a completely safe life was no life at all.

Before him, the crowd of well-wishers seemed to rearrange themselves, and all at once the Codys were in their places on the wagons, waving good-bye.

Sitting proudly upright in the saddle, Bill urged Orion to the head of the procession.

"Good-bye, Mary! Good-bye, Martha!" called excited voices as the carriage began to move forward.

Bill glanced back at the womenfolk, who looked like royalty in the brightly polished carriage, with its finely upholstered interior. Anticipating the audience of neighbors, Martha had made sure all her sisters were wearing their best dresses. The two horses pulling the carriage, Little Gray and Baker, looked like a team of Thoroughbreds in their jangly silver trappings. Bill thought he could do without all that luxury, and perhaps even without one or two of his sisters, though he knew he didn't mean that last. He longed to urge Orion to a trot as they pulled onto Main Street, but their friends and neighbors were still keeping up with them, waving and calling their endless good-byes. The silliness of it all, he thought. As if a good-bye could matter. It couldn't make a friendship last any longer.

Main Street paralleled the Mississippi, and they would follow the river all the way to Davenport, some fifteen miles south. As they crossed over Wisconsin Street, Bill looked east toward the riverbank for one last glimpse of the Green Tree.

What he saw made him look twice.

A small figure, unmistakably Joe's, stood in front of the tree leaping up and down and waving toward the river. Behind him, majestic on the swells, loomed the steamer *Polar Star*. As Joe jumped and gestured, the steamer's whistle opened up suddenly in a chorus of joyful shrieks. Bill could see the steamboatmen gathered on the deck, waving their hats in the air as the whistle continued to blow.

No boy could ever have received such an

honorable farewell. Bill rose in his stirrups and waved and hurrahed with all his might until Joe grew smaller and smaller, and the steamboat's whistle faded away. Still casting an occasional backward glance, Bill changed his mind and decided that perhaps good-byes did matter. That the right good-byes might matter more than anything else.

Chapter Three

UNDER WAY AT LAST

★ ★ ★

Every muscle in Bill's body screamed for mercy. He had felt all right the night before, when they had reached Davenport, where they were to overnight with an old stagecoaching friend of Pa's. He had felt fine at the table, eating Mrs. Alexander's roast chicken and potatoes as Pa held forth on the blessings and bounties awaiting them in the new territories. He had even been comfortable

enough squashed into a bed between the two Alexander boys, whom he had never liked before and now liked even less.

But this morning was a different matter. Knives stabbed at the backs of his legs with each step he took. Iron bands contracted around his lower back and cinched themselves tight. There was a kraut grater on the inside of each knee, rubbing in merciless circles. On his entire body, Bill decided, his elbows were the only things that didn't hurt.

He'd ridden plenty in his life. Who'd have thought ten hours in the saddle would be so different from two? Was he going to feel like this every day until they reached Uncle Elijah's? He worried about Orion as well. One way or the other, the horse was going to have to walk to Missouri with the rest of them. But was Bill making things too difficult for the horse by insisting on riding him the whole way?

"What's wrong with you?" Julia whispered, standing by the kitchen table as she pinned her hair up in a bun. It was a fancy trick, as she did it while balancing Mary Hannah on one hip.

Ma and Pa were outside helping the Alexanders with the chores, and Martha was in the back room scrubbing her sisters' faces with a vengeance. Julia was the only person in the world, except maybe for Joe, in whom Bill was willing to confide.

"My legs and back hurt something awful!" he

whispered. "I could barely sit down at breakfast."

Julia gazed at her brother with sympathy.

"Can't hardly believe we've only been gone one day. And I reckon it's only going to get worse today," Bill added ruefully.

"We could swap places," Julia said. "You could sit in the carriage holding Mary Hannah and answering Nellie every minute when she asks why this, why that. And I could ride Orion."

Mary Hannah's pudgy hand found Julia's braid and gave it a tug, as if in protest.

"You'd have to wear my britches," Bill said, pretending to consider this seriously.

Nellie, who had heard her name, shot into the room and wrapped her arms around Julia's leg.

"Dulia," she cooed.

"Yes, I would," Julia said, in an equally solemn tone, rubbing the top of her little sister's head. "And I'll need a rifle, of course, in case I see something that needs shooting."

"You'd best coil a rope onto the saddle, too, so if we catch a bandit, you can pull him along behind you," Bill said. Julia nodded.

"Okay, then," Bill said. "Will you tell Ma and Pa, or shall I?"

"Tell Ma and Pa what?" came Ma's voice from the doorway.

"Bill gonna catch a bannit on Orion!" Nellie

shouted, bursting with pride.

"Bill's going to what?" asked Ma, the familiar look of worry coming over her face.

"Oh, Ma," said Bill quickly. "You know how muddled Nellie gets about everything."

Ma looked from Bill to Julia, and Bill made his face look as innocent as possible. He didn't think he could stand it if Ma was going to start worrying this early in the morning.

"Come along, then," she finally said. "The sun's almost up, and we've a long day ahead of us. Where's Martha?"

"Fussing over Eliza Alice, Ma," Julia said. Bill rolled his eyes. It was a puzzle to him why Martha thought it so important to look tidy when all one had to do the livelong day was bounce around on a carriage seat. Julia didn't think it was important. That was one of the reasons she was his favorite sister.

"I'll get them," Ma said. "Now outside, both of you."

The sun was just coming up as Bill and Julia stepped out into the cool morning. Though they didn't have two thousand miles to travel, as did the gold seekers heading for California, Pa was determined they make good time. If they rose each morning by four-thirty and ate and washed quickly, they could travel fifteen miles before stopping for the night. At that rate, Pa had said, they would cross into Missouri in roughly three weeks.

Neither Bill nor Julia had much of a head for geography, but when Pa explained their course in terms of the stagecoach routes, they could understand it better. LeClaire was on the eastern border of Iowa, just about halfway up the state. Missouri was the state directly below. Pa planned to follow the stage routes west from county seat to county seat, until they had crossed half of Iowa. Then they would turn south into Missouri and head west again until they reached Weston, where Pa's brother, Elijah, lived.

Bill didn't mind getting up so early. This trip was the most exciting thing to happen to him in a long time, and he wanted each day to last as long as possible. Though the way his muscles protested as he walked to Orion made him realize this day, at least, would feel very long. He examined Orion anxiously, paying special attention to his hooves, but the horse seemed perfectly fine. Turk was also looking bright-eyed and eager to get under way. So Bill saddled up Orion as if he hadn't a care in the world. Wouldn't catch Kit Carson moaning and groaning, he thought to himself. So I won't neither.

"My, but it's brisk this morning!" Pa said, striding back and forth between the wagons as he checked over their gear.

"It sure is, Pa," Bill called.

"Wouldn't be the first time Iowa saw snow in May," said George Yancey, his powerful hands fastening the yoke to his team of oxen.

"Stuff and nonsense," said Mr. Alexander as he helped Martha and Eliza Alice into the carriage. "If anything falls from the sky today, it'll be rain, I promise. These old bones don't lie."

"I'm sure they don't, Edward," Ma said, climbing up alongside Martha. "But I do hope it stays clear today all the same."

As had happened the day before in LeClaire, what seemed a chaos of horses, grown-ups, and children suddenly turned itself into an orderly expedition, ready to depart. The two Alexander boys stood in the doorway of the house, their normally taunting faces looking downright green with envy as Bill walked Orion in circles, letting the horse stretch out his legs.

"We'd best be off if we've any hope of reaching Muscatine by tomorrow," boomed Pa's voice. "Thanks again, Alexander, for all your hospitality."

The girls' voices joined in thanks, and Bill could feel his mother's eyes on him.

"Thank you, sir. Thank you, ma'am," Bill said politely to Mr. and Mrs. Alexander. "Good-bye, Franklin. Good-bye, Thomas. Have fun in school," he couldn't resist adding, pleased with the scowls the boys made in response.

The grown-up Alexanders beamed and waved at the departing family. Though his aches were the worse for his being back in the saddle, Bill was happy to be on the move again. Clouds were beginning to thicken overhead, and it was chilly, but Bill didn't care. Was there anything better in the world than being on horseback and heading west?

There was some kind of commotion ahead. Bill leaned forward in his saddle, and as the Cody wagons moved closer, he could see it was a stagecoach. Bill's body had gone more or less numb beneath his wet clothes. He barely even noticed the drops anymore. Ma was convinced he would catch cold, and she had tried and tried to get him to join the girls in the carriage, where it was dry, but Bill refused. He didn't want to miss anything, and now he was glad he'd stuck it out. The rain had been falling steadily since before lunch, turning the roads into infamous Iowa mud. Ahead, the stage had blundered into a deep pool of it, and it was stuck fast. Bill turned Orion and had the horse trot over to Pa's wagon.

"There's a stage mired down, Pa," Bill called.

"Best go see if they can use a hand," Pa called back, and he motioned to George and Ma to slow up behind him.

Proud to be asked to scout ahead, Bill rode closer.

It was a Concord, brightly painted red, its steps and luggage railing a glossy black. Hitched to a six-horse team, the coach was oval in shape, with real glass windows, and the top was flattened to carry luggage. From behind it Bill could see the coach's triangular covered boot was packed tightly with baggage.

The occupants, three men and a woman, were standing at the side of the road as the driver examined the wheels. The mud looked to be almost two feet deep in some places. The worst of it pooled at the bottom of a slight incline, where the stagecoach now sat. But it was growing slicker on the road, too, and as Orion walked, Bill could hear a sucking sound as each hoof came up. Turk had given up and sat at the road's edge.

Bill returned to Pa. "It's stuck good," he said with some satisfaction. "The mud's real deep."

Pa shouted and motioned, and following his orders, the carriage and both wagons pulled off the road and onto the grass.

"I've got a couple of fence rails in the wagon," Pa said. "Help me get 'em out. George, come give me a hand, will you?"

Bill swung off the horse.

"Don't you fret, Orion," he murmured, rubbing the animal's neck reassuringly. "We're just gonna help these folks out for a spell. Nothing you need to bother yourself about." Then he turned to Turk, who was regarding him seriously with his huge yellow eyes. "Now you need to stay with Orion, understand? Those horses down there are spooked enough already. They catch sight of you, that might just be the end of 'em. Stay, Turk." Turk stayed, and Bill knew he wouldn't have to tell him again.

Together, Bill, George, and Pa carried the boards down the slick incline toward the stagecoach. The little group turned to watch them approach, their faces showing they could hardly believe their luck.

"Looks like you all could use a hand," Pa called in his thundery voice.

"Slough got us, sure enough," said the driver, referring to the valleys in the prairie that collected rain and bred mud in bad weather. "Certainly appreciate the help, mister."

"Used to drive a stage myself," Pa said. "Let's see what we can do about this, eh?"

"It's high time someone did something helpful around here," came a shrill voice.

"Will you once and for all hush up, Darla?" said a man's voice, exasperated.

Ma had told Bill a hundred times it was rude to stare and even ruder to eavesdrop. But he simply could not help himself.

The woman who had spoken was standing several yards from the coach, up to her ankles in mud. In spite of the ugly scowl on her face, she was quite pretty and didn't look much older than Martha. Her fashionable dress was soaking wet, and there was mud all over the bottom of her petticoats. In one hand she held a birdcage. The other rested firmly on her hip.

"'Take a steamer,' Daddy said. 'Take a steamer and pay the extra,'" she was now saying. "'You'll get there twice as fast,' he said. But would you listen? No you would not. Just like your penny-pinching folks in Scotland, anything to save a few dollars!"

With that, she whacked the man nearest her on the arm with the birdcage. The two other men just shook their heads and rolled their eyes. Bill imagined they had heard a good bit more of the same already.

"Come on, men," Pa called to them. "We're going to need all of you, and you, too, Bill, to move this coach!"

Bill couldn't help glancing around to see if the other men had noticed how casually Pa had included him, as if he were grown-up, too.

The driver seemed relieved to let Pa take the lead, and climbed back into his seat. Gathering the other men around, Pa explained that they would wedge and brace the fence rails under the wheels while the driver urged the horses forward. The men surrounded the stage and pushed the wooden boards into the mud under the wheels as the driver urged the horses forward.

The stagecoach moved slightly, but the horses kept slipping and couldn't pull hard enough to dislodge the wheels from the mud.

"You're well and truly stuck here," called Pa finally. "Get in any deeper and you'll need a team of oxen to pull you out. Best unload the luggage and give it another try. Taking off the extra weight just might make the difference."

The driver hopped up lightly onto the stage roof and began to untie the trunks piled up there, while Bill helped the other men pull carpetbags from the boot.

By now the mud, which had the consistency of greasy brown dough, had congealed around Bill's boots and ankles, and the rain had soaked him thoroughly, but he didn't mind a bit. He felt proud of Pa, of his willingness to help people he didn't know and would probably never see again. He loved watching Pa take control and delighted in the way even the driver deferred immediately to him. All of them understood, as folks always seemed to, how capable Pa was. All of them, that is, except Darla.

"What in land's end are you doing?" she screeched as the carpet bags were tossed one by one onto the wet grass. The sky gave a rumble, and the rain began to fall harder.

"There's too much weight on the stage," Pa called out when no one else answered. He was staggering slightly under the weight of a trunk. "Got to lighten the load."

"Not with my baggage you don't!" cried Darla. She moved forward as if to stop Pa but slipped in the mud and landed with a wet thud on her behind, dropping the birdcage. Bill bit back a laugh. All the men ignored her and continued to unload the stage, except for her husband.

"Are you all right?" he called. "Do you need help?"

"Do not speak to me!" she shouted at him. "You of all people are no help! Look at this mess you've gotten us in." Her husband shrugged and turned away as one of the other men said softly, "Looks like she's the one in the mess."

Skating carefully through the slick wet earth, Bill offered her a hand. He thought it was something Pa would have done if he hadn't had his own hands full.

"Keep your hands off of me!" she said shrilly.

"It's all the same to me, ma'am," Bill replied, backing away. Sorry old puss, who did she think she was? Bill didn't mind being sassed, but he thought Pa was due plenty of respect, and he certainly wasn't getting any from her. Let her sit in the mud then, Bill thought.

Soon all the baggage was on the ground, and they were ready to try again.

"Bill," Pa said, "and you, Miss . . ." Darla's husband murmured something to Pa. "Mrs. Dawson. I'll need the two of you to calm the horses and to hold their heads when I give the word."

Bill went toward the mired team, but Mrs. Dawson, who had struggled to her feet on her own, simply snorted.

"I'll do no such thing!" she exclaimed, picking up her birdcage and brandishing it in front of her like a weapon. "I am a lady, not a stagecoach hand."

Bill thought he had never seen Pa so exasperated.

"Julia can do it, Pa," Bill said quickly. "She's as strong as me, almost, and not afraid of horses."

Pa nodded, and Bill raced up the slippery hill toward the carriage.

"What on earth is going on?" Ma asked as Bill poked his wet and dripping head inside.

"William Frederick, watch yourself!" cried Martha, scrunching against Eliza Alice to keep from being dripped on.

"They're sunk deep in the mud, almost up over the wheels," Bill said. "And the driver doesn't seem to know a thing about what to do, and Pa's telling everybody how to help out, but there's a lady there and she won't do a thing but complain and Pa sent me to see if Julia could come help."

Bill almost felt like fainting away after getting that whole sentence out without taking a breath. Julia, forgetting where she was, tried to leap to her feet and hit her head on the roof of the coach.

"Julia, my goodness!" Ma said.

"Ouch!" cried Nellie, who always had sympathy

to spare for her older sister.

Julia rubbed her head but said, "I'm all right. May I go, Ma? Please?"

The rain pummeled the roof of the carriage and fell down Bill's back as they all watched their mother.

"You'll ruin your dress," Eliza Alice said primly. "Your hair will kink."

"And likely catch your death of cold," Martha added. "Ma, Pa must simply do without more help, mustn't he?"

Bill had no use for this kind of foolishness.

"They're really stuck, Ma, and sinking fast," he said, in as grown-up a voice as he could muster. "And you know Pa won't leave till they're safe and out. May Julia come, please?"

The thought of the entire family having to stay put until the stage was safe kept Martha from making any further objections. Ma gave a small nod, and with a distinctly unladylike cry, Julia clambered over Ma and leaped out of the carriage, landing in the mud with a satisfying squish. Bill was so glad Julia was joining him that he even let her hold his hand for support.

"I never dreamed she'd say yes!" Julia said as they ran toward the stagecoach. "But you always know what to say, clever Bill!"

Bill shrugged, but inside he felt pleased. It *had* been smart to tell Ma they'd be stuck as long as the coach was. And true, too, because that was just what Pa would do.

Bill and Julia quickly took their positions in front of the team. Julia was practically giddy with excitement.

"What are their names?" Bill called up to the stage driver, who was standing nearby. The driver looked confused. "The two lead horses. What are their names?"

The driver shook his head like he thought Bill was crazy, but he answered anyway.

"Kip an' Collin."

"Kip and Collin," Bill repeated. He hadn't asked just for fun. The horses were getting more frightened the longer they were stuck in the mud. But Bill knew that every horse knows its own name, and spoken in a quiet and encouraging way, the sound of it could have a calming effect.

"Just keep saying their names to 'em," Bill said to Julia, and she nodded.

"Everybody ready?" Pa called. "Okay. Now! Go! Go!"

The men with the fence rails thrust all their weight onto the boards, forcing the rails down and under the sinking wheels. The driver, standing to one side of the horses, shouted and whipped the team, urging them forward. Keeping the horses' heads up, Julia and Bill encouraged them to go ahead.

"Good, Kip. Good, Collin," they kept repeating.

"Harder! Harder! Here she comes!"

There was a jolt and a loud squelch, and the stage suddenly pulled free and lurched forward. Bill and Julia leaped safely out of the way as the team of horses lunged ahead. Running alongside, the driver had the horses advance twenty or thirty feet over the grass just off the road before coming to a stop on drier ground.

All the men, including the driver, applauded Pa. Bill thought he would burst with pride, and no one clapped louder than he did himself.

"There's likely more mud ahead," Pa warned, waving off the applause. "Go around if you can, and keep the coach as light as possible. Your passengers best walk a spell."

"Walk?" cried an outraged Mrs. Dawson. "I'm a paying ticketholder! I'll not walk a step!"

The stage driver produced a soggy piece of paper from his pocket and waved it at her.

"In case you forgot," he said. "Your leaflet of do's and don't's, which was issued to every one of ya before we started out . . ." With everyone looking at him, he lost his train of thought for a moment.

"Is that," he continued suddenly, "number four, sayin' when the driver asks you to get off and walk, do so without grumblin', which is right afore the part about not jumpin' off the coach if the team runs away, better to take your chances than to get squished under the wheels."

It was the most he'd said during the entire ordeal.

Mrs. Dawson trembled with rage. "Do something," she hissed at her husband.

Bill snuck a look at Mr. Dawson, who seemed to have suddenly lost the use of his hearing.

"You're the one who got us into this mess!" she shouted at the driver. "You're supposed to be a professional. Would you *mind* telling me how you explain this?"

"I'd be *happy* to explain," the driver shouted, stomping his little foot into the mud. "It so happens I ain't never *drove* no stagecoach across no prairie before! That answer your question, ma'am?"

Bill was laughing so hard, he almost knocked Julia down. Pa tugged at his son's elbow.

"Come on, children. Nothing else we can help these folks with, and the day's getting on."

As they came up the hill, the sound of Mrs. Dawson's voice following them, the door to the carriage opened and Ma leaned out, holding a blanket for Julia. She wrapped it around herself and climbed back into the coach. She immediately stuck her head out the window.

"Oh, Bill," she whispered, her eyes shining. "Wasn't that exciting?"

It hadn't been a cyclone or an attack by wild wolves, but Bill had to agree it had been pretty exciting. After all, even Kit Carson had to start somewhere.

CHAPTER FOUR

THE INN

★ ★ ★

Just over a week into their journey, near Oscaloosa, they enjoyed their first paid lodgings, a stagecoach stop known simply as the Inn. Papa told them he'd heard the Inn, a generously sized stone building, boasted its own storeroom that held flour, sugar, and cheese; ample areas to graze and rest stock; comfortable guest rooms; and a

long dining room where tired travelers could refresh themselves with a hot meal. Bill would have been happier camping out of doors, but he immediately changed his mind when he learned the Inn had its own stone jailhouse, where prisoners being transported aboard stagecoaches could be safely held overnight. As soon as she learned this, Ma declared that they would have to continue on to the next town, until the cheerful innkeeper assured her that the jailhouse was quite empty and that no inmates were expected on the incoming stage.

The Inn sat just off the road. Pa had gone inside to settle their arrangements with the innkeeper, and Ma and the girls stood in the lush, warm grass near the front door, enjoying the spring sun and stretching their legs, while George unyoked the oxen. Julia joined Bill, who was standing a short way off by the building's corner, looking toward the back of the property.

"The jail's back there," Bill said with a gleam in his eye.

"The innkeeper said it was empty," Julia said.

"Course he would *say* that," Bill said, "so as not to scare paying customers off. Could be packed to the brim with any number of dastardly characters, and we'd never be the wiser. 'Less they escape, that is."

Bill slid his eyes sideways at his sister

and was gratified to see her give a little shudder.

"Anyhow, me and Turk aim to go have a look," he continued. "You coming?"

Julia hesitated.

"Oh, well, stay here then," Bill said, trying to sound like he didn't care. "Sometimes I forget you're a girl."

"I'm coming!" Julia retorted indignantly, pushing her way past her brother.

"Bill, for the last time, do not wander!" Ma called from where she was standing on the grass. Bill obediently stopped, but he almost groaned with frustration.

"And Julia," Ma continued, "you know you're supposed to be keeping an eye on Nellie and Mary Hannah."

"Yes, Ma," Julia called sweetly, stopping in her tracks. But to Bill she said, "Really, it's enough to drive a person mad!"

"It's only because she knows this Inn is seething with bad influences," Bill answered back, his eyes brightening at the thought of it. "There could be horse thieves coming in, Julia, or even murderers. Bandits could be watching us right now, planning to ambush us when we set out in the morning. We could be lodging next to mountain men and never know until we saw their rifles! In that very stage," Bill continued, gesturing at a distant coach making its way down the road toward them, "could be Jim Bridger himself!"

Bill felt a little thrill thinking of him, the greatest mountain man ever, excepting, of course, Kit Carson himself.

But Julia was shaking her head. "What would Jim Bridger want in these parts? Black's Fork must be a thousand miles away," she said, referring to Bridger's famous Green River trading post.

Bill shook his head. "A man like Jim Bridger is needed everywhere," he said gravely. "Much as he might like to spend his whole life in the mountains, trapping beaver and wrestling bears, duty will eventually call and he will answer. When the army has a need to send an expedition over the California hills exploring, who's the best man to call to show the way and keep the troops safe? Jim Bridger, that's who."

"Horses!" called Nellie, dashing over to Julia and excitedly tugging her skirt. With a start, Julia suddenly remembered her two young charges. She grabbed Nellie's hand and looked around for Mary Hannah. The little girl was nowhere in sight.

"Mary Hannah!" she said frantically. "Bill, she's gone!"

"Julia, she can't even crawl yet," Bill said, impatient that his mountain-man reverie had been interrupted. "She's not old enough to get herself lost."

"But she's old enough to get herself abducted!" Julia cried.

"Mary Hannah ducked!" shouted Nellie, eager to help sound the alarm.

Turk leaped to his feet at the sound of raised voices, ready to protect Bill and his sisters. Julia shushed Nellie, but the sound of her voice had already attracted the attention of Martha, who was coming out of the Inn's front door. Bill resisted the impulse to say "I told you so" to Julia as Martha came striding toward them with Mary Hannah safely on her hip.

"Nellie, for heaven's sake, lower your voice!" said Martha in a low, practiced tone. "Honestly, Julia, you're supposed to be watching both of them, and you're not even taking proper care of one."

Bill expected his sister to retort angrily at this, but Julia just nodded vigorously and look relieved.

"You're right, Martha," she said, taking the sleepy Mary Hannah into her arms. "This is no place to forget oneself."

Martha looked surprised at the unusually agreeable demeanor of her wild young sister, but she returned to Eliza Alice, who was still waiting by the carriage with Ma.

On the road the stage that had been the topic of so much discussion came to a halt nearby. Bill did not really expect Jim Bridger to be inside, but he was nonetheless disappointed when the door opened and out stepped Darla Dawson.

He only had time to give Julia a meaningful nudge before Pa emerged cheerfully from the Inn.

"We're all set," he said, clapping his hands together. "And if even half the stories I heard about this place are true, we'll dine like kings tonight!"

Judging from the tightness of his waistband, Bill had to agree with what Pa had heard about the Inn's cooking. After three helpings of beef stew—swimming with chunks of good, rich meat, carrots, onions, and potato—four squares of cornbread, and two and a half large slices of apple pie, Bill leaned back in his chair and admitted defeat. He felt the slight pressure of Turk's nose nudging his leg underneath the table, and making sure that Ma was looking in the other direction, he slipped the dog a little piece of pie. The long, smoky dining room had grown dark, but the orange glow from the enormous hearth fire gave it a cozy feel. The men from the once-mired stagecoach stood around the fire with glasses of ale. Some other men Bill hadn't seen before sat eating their dinner in silence. The Codys were all gathered together at one end of the table. Much to Bill's dismay, Martha had asked Darla Dawson to join them. She and Martha now had their heads together and murmured seriously to each other.

"And how are we all this fine evening?" boomed the innkeeper with a strange, lilting accent as he bustled into the dining room.

"Well indeed," said Pa. "And if your beds are as good as this stew, we'll sleep like babes!"

Several of the men nodded in agreement, and the innkeeper beamed.

"It's the wife's family recipe," he said. "From the Blasket Isles, back in Ireland. Some say the Inn is famous throughout Iowa for it, though it did a good enough business before the wife and I took it over. They say Kit Carson himself once stayed here, but I can't say for sure, as that was before my time."

Bill shot to attention at the mention of his hero. Kit Carson, here in this inn! Why, maybe he'd sat in the very chair Bill was in right now!

"Carson," said one of the men by the fire. "Now there's a fella. I heard the president made him Indian agent for the whole of New Mexico Territory."

Bill had heard that, too. He stiffened with pride on Kit's behalf. The New Mexico Territory was enormous, and there were more isolated Indian tribes there than anywhere else in the country. The Indian agent had to be a man the Indians respected and trusted. It was his job to settle disputes, look out for the Indians' welfare, keep the peace, and act as liaison between the tribes and the U.S.

government. For settlers, army officers, and Indians alike, the Indian agent was an important man indeed. No wonder they'd asked Kit Carson to take on this job.

"Y'all heard the one about the Mexican War, right?" asked another.

Heard about it, thought Bill. Who on earth could have failed to hear how Kit and a single soldier had crawled two miles on their stomachs over rocky terrain to break through enemy lines and bring Colonel Kearney's request for reinforcements safely to San Diego?

"Yeah, I heard it," said a darkly bearded man sitting at the table.

"What about the one where the two grizzlies treed him outside of Jim Bridger's camp?" asked another man with a grin.

Hardly something to make light of, Bill thought, bristling. Miles from help, his rifle lying thirty feet below in the undergrowth and two angry grizzly bears of outlandish proportions climbing the tree after him, only Kit Carson would have had the strength and presence of mind to cut a stout branch with his hunting knife and fashion it into a club before the bears could reach him. Only Kit Carson could have fought those bears off for over two hours while clinging to the tree, striking the attacking bears on the nose each time they lunged.

“I don’t believe a word of it,” said the bearded man.

“What’s that?” said one of the men from the stage, looking up and down the table to see who had spoken.

“I said,” the bearded man repeated as he got to his feet, “I don’t believe a word of it. Ain’t no man could do half the things they say Carson done. Like as not it’s all a bunch of nonsense.”

Some of the men laughed, and others like Pa simply shook their heads. Bill was rigid with outrage. From across the table, Julia shot her brother a look of sympathetic anger.

The bearded man continued. “Either he’s the biggest liar since Davy Crockett or he chooses to keep his mouth shut while other folks lie for him. Either way, ’tain’t none of it true. Man like that, living in the mountains with animals and savages, a person can’t listen to a thing comin’ out of his mouth. No, Kit Carson’s nothin’ more than a grizzly in a ratty buckskin suit. I’d cut him down soon as look at him.”

Somebody had to speak up. Someone had to defend Kit Carson and stand up to these men. Well, he would do it. Wasn’t he almost nine? Bill opened his mouth to do so.

“That is an outrageous misstatement, for which I insist you apologize.”

For a second Bill thought he had spoken. But everyone turned away from him. Bill looked, too, and his mouth hung so far open he resembled an astonished catfish, for the person who had stood up in Kit's defense was his sister Martha!

"I had the privilege of meeting Mr. Carson when I was a small child visiting Missouri," Martha continued. "He was a thorough gentleman. He neither drinks nor smokes nor gambles. He treats women with respect and comports himself with manners becoming the finest class of citizen. None present shall speak ill of him."

Bill's own surprise was reflected in the faces of the men around the fire and tables. Only Pa looked amused. Ma was pointedly ignoring the entire proceedings, steadily spooning stew into Nellie's mouth.

"I certainly meant no offense, ma'am," said the bearded man at last, looking uncomfortable. "I do apologize."

Martha gave a satisfied nod and sat down. Pa joined the men by the fire; Bill heard them laughing as they asked him about his outspoken daughter.

As for Bill, he was aching to ask Martha a thousand questions, but she was engrossed again with Darla Dawson and he couldn't get her attention. Martha and Kit Carson! Why had he never been told? He thought he would burst with impatience as he kept staring at Martha, who would just not look at him. Ma finally took pity on him and offered a few details.

"It was around 1840," she said. "Your pa and I were fixing to get married. Martha's own ma had died some five years earlier, and Martha stayed at Uncle Elijah's in Missouri while Pa came to Cleveland to collect me and my things. She saw Mr. Carson there, had a little talk with him. That's all I know."

"But why didn't anyone ever *tell* me?" Bill spluttered.

"I expect because you never asked," she replied.

Bill rolled his eyes. Wasn't that just like a grown-up? How could a body be expected to ask a question when he doesn't know one should even be asked?

"Ma," Bill said suddenly. "Just so's I know. Have *you* ever met Kit Carson?"

Ma allowed herself a small smile. "No, William, I have not," she replied.

"I'll be more careful about checking from now on," he said. He suddenly noticed that he was the only male at the table. All the other men, including Pa, were at the other end of the dining room. He got to his feet and murmured to Turk to stay put.

The night had grown chilly, and the fire was roaring hotly. Standing around it, the men had let their conversation turn to politics. They didn't seem to notice Bill as he took a place at Pa's side. Pa was telling the men about their eventual destination of Kansas Territory, and the men were full of questions and suggestions.

"I hear the land is rich," one of them said. "But you'll want a claim close to the fort. There's good trading there, and the steamers visit every day. Trees, plenty of water. Protection, too, of course."

"The bill pass yet?" another asked, and Pa shook his head. This was the bill Pa had talked about on their last night in LeClaire. Bill thought it sure seemed to be taking a long time. The whole thing seemed simple enough. Either the government would let the settlers decide on the slavery issue themselves, or they'd say the new territories couldn't have slaves. What was so complicated that it took all these months to sort out? Especially when it meant families like theirs couldn't legally claim their land until the matter was settled.

"But it will soon," Pa was saying. "And when it passes, I'll be there, ready to stake my claim."

"Lotta folks heading for the new territories," said the bearded man. "I hear there's societies back east that are sending volunteers to settle the territories, just so they can vote against slavery."

"I hear the same," said a man Bill recognized as Mr. Dawson. "And the proslavers have the same idea. They're paying any man who'll take the money to go settle and cast a vote for a slave state."

"What are you, Cody?" asked the stage driver. "Proslavery or Free-Soiler?"

"Neither," Pa replied. "The question has nothing to do with me. I'm a farmer, going to Kansas to break the land and get my hands into that rich earth where they say anything'll grow."

"Well, you *gotta* feel one way or the other," said the bearded man.

"I'm a settler, not a politician," said Pa calmly. "It's none of my concern. Let those who feel strongly about it do as they will."

"I don't know," said Mr. Dawson. "Some people think it could get real ugly."

"Maybe," said Pa. He sounded firm when he added, "But not for the Codys. We don't aim to be any part of it."

"Well, best of luck to you," said the bearded man.

"Thanks," said Pa. "I'm Isaac Cody. I don't believe I caught your name."

"Griggs is the name," the man replied. "Call me Sammy."

And Bill's world suddenly stopped. His quiet enjoyment of the fire's warmth, his contentment at his father's reassurances, evaporated at the sound of that name. He realized with a rush that he had not thought of his brother Sammy, not once, since the morning they had left LeClaire eight days ago. He felt weak with his own treason. He had broken his promise to Sammy.

"Can you believe it?" Julia was at his side.

"I can't," Bill said glumly, amazed how Julia was thinking exactly the same thing.

"Our proper, boring Martha defending Kit Carson in front of a tavern full of men. Who'd have thought it?"

What Martha had done, so amazing and startling before, seemed so unimportant now. Bill shook his head.

"I ain't thought of him once since we left home, Julia."

"Kit Carson?" she asked, confused.

"Sammy," he replied. She looked surprised, then chagrined. Bill knew he wasn't the only Cody who'd forgotten about Sammy. Had they all? Did they just need to go a mile or two from home for all their memories of Sammy to disappear as if he'd never even existed?

The thought upset Bill so much that he had to leave the dining room before another second went by.

Chapter Five

MISSOURI

"Is this Misery?" Nellie asked.

Pa laughed and hoisted his second-youngest daughter into his arms. "Missouri, Nellie-belle. We are now in Miz-Oo-Ree. See that line of little trees to the west? That'll be the west fork of Big Creek. By suppertime, we'll be on the other side of it."

Bill thought it was about as far from misery as a place could be. After almost three weeks, they finally had left Iowa behind and, just this morning, crossed into a state Bill had never seen before.

They had stopped the wagons to give the oxen and horses a rest. There was not a cloud to be seen from one end of the horizon to the other, and the sun overhead blazed to its fullest. The earth seemed to overflow with everything spring had to offer. In all directions the prairie gently swelled and undulated, its carpet of grass and wildflowers rippling in the breeze.

"It's a sight, ain't it?" Pa said, catching the look of wonder that had crossed his son's face. Bill could only nod, unable to take his eyes off the ocean of wild grass and the tantalizing horizon far beyond, promising all that was new and unknown.

"What do you say, Mary, shall we have ourselves a picnic?"

"I think we'll have a mutiny on our hands if we don't," Ma said, already spreading a blanket over the grass.

"That's the best news I heard all day," said George Yancey, turning loose the two teams of oxen, still in their yokes, to let them graze. "I got myself a powerful hunger, I do."

Bill grinned at Julia, standing nearby, and she grinned back. From what they had observed so far, there wasn't a single moment in the day when George did not have himself a powerful hunger. It was a fortunate thing George planned to go straight home after the Codys were settled on their claim. Bill had guessed there wasn't enough game in the whole of Kansas Territory to keep George's stomach full.

"Julia, I could use a little help," Ma said, and

Julia's face fell. Bill knew Ma wasn't supposed to have to ask for help. Julia should have spread out the blanket herself, should now be unloading the dinnerware and unwrapping the cheese. As she had told Bill many times, she did try to be good, and she did honestly want to please Ma. But the world was so full of exciting things, Bill and Julia both knew she would never live up to Martha of the low voice and exquisite manners. Martha, who seemed always to know what was right and proper, and who, in her infuriating way, actually preferred to be ladylike.

"Sorry, Ma," Julia said, leaving Bill's side and beginning to unload the plates and cups from the back of the prairie schooner. "Sit a spell and enjoy the view. I'll ready everything."

Bill sat down on the woolen blanket and Pa sat down beside him. Martha deposited Mary Hannah on his left and sat herself down with Nellie and Eliza Alice on either side of her. They were a good-sized family, but even sitting together, all eight of them, with enormous George to boot, they seemed a tiny, insignificant speck on the immense ocean of land.

"It's a big country, ain't it, Pa?" said Bill.

"And it holds everything a family needs," Pa said, as Julia passed around the bread wrapped in a piece of old linen. "Our government is giving us a real gift. I hope you know that. Prime farmland, as wide and empty as the summer sky, and just a dollar and a quarter an acre. All we need to do is build our home, and farm the land and live on it. That's not much to ask of a man for a hundred acres of pure opportunity, is it?"

"No, sir," said Bill. "Sounds almost too good to be true."

"But it is true," Pa said, his wide smile breaking through his beard. "And we have President Pierce to thank, opening up these lands and entrusting them to families like ours. With hard work and good weather, there's nothing we won't have, Bill. You'll see."

Bill loved the way Pa was talking to him, almost man to man. He had treated Sammy this way sometimes, treating him as if he were a grown-up. Sammy had always looked so big and proud at those times, using a funny gruff voice to respond to Pa's remarks. The thought of Sammy created a little ache in Bill's chest, and he concentrated on Pa instead, searching for a way to draw out the conversation.

"What about this thing folks keep talking about, Pa?" he asked at last. "This compromise thing?"

Bill noticed that Ma glanced over toward them as she poured some water into a tin cup and passed it to him. Ma rarely joined in talk of politics, but she always seemed to be listening especially carefully when the topic was raised.

"It's nothing we need to worry ourselves over,

son. It's true that there are men who feel pretty strongly that these new territories should allow slaves, and there are men who feel the opposite just as strongly. And maybe they each intend to make it their business and see to it they get their own way. But we're not freedom fighters from back east, Bill. We're farmers. My politicking days are long gone. Let them have it out amongst themselves. Either way, it won't make our crops grow any faster."

Pa never talked much about what he called his politicking days. Bill knew Pa had been elected as a representative in the Iowa legislature three or four years back but had never actually served in the position. There had been some sort of disagreement following the election, when Pa had been told by some businessmen how he was to vote on certain issues and the like. Whatever had exactly happened, it had left a bad taste in Pa's mouth, and he had ended up declining the position altogether. He'd been wary of politics and politicians ever since.

"What exactly is supposed to happen?" asked Julia, suddenly joining the conversation. Bill knew it wasn't considered ladylike to be interested in politics, but Julia had just asked the very question on his mind.

"Once the bill has passed and the territories are open, the new settlers will choose their land and file their claims. Then there'll be a vote on whether or not Kansas should be a slave state, and each man will have his say, yes or no. Majority rules, so whichever side gets the most votes will win. And that'll be that."

"Might not be so easy, Mr. Cody," said George, taking an enormous bite of cheese. "This Senator Atchison the Missourians elected is a real firebrand, and folks listen to him. I hear talk he won't stop at nothing to make sure Kansas is a slave state, same as Missouri."

"But what has Missouri got to do with it?" asked Bill. "Why should their senator care one way or the other about Kansas?"

"Your uncle Elijah says Missouri thinks of the Kansas Territory as its backyard, more or less," Pa explained. "They're going to want the new state to permit slavery, too. That way they have the choice of settling in Kansas and bringing their slaves along. Also, Elijah says slaveowners in Missouri figure all their slaves will be running away to hide in Kansas if it's made a free state."

Bill thought the whole thing sounded more and more confusing each minute.

"I heard that, too," George said with his mouth partially full. "That's why I think there's gonna be trouble, and men'll be stoppin' at nothin' to make sure they get their way."

"What can they do, George?" asked Pa. "A vote's a vote. Oh, I expect there'll be some ballot stuffing and things of that sort on both sides. But it'll all balance out in the end."

"All I'm saying is it might not be that simple," said George, but he was more interested in a second helping of cheese than in pursuing the topic and didn't elaborate.

"Well, you ain't the first man to disagree with me, George, and I reckon you won't be the last. That's another great thing about this country. Room enough for every man's view. Don't you worry about a thing, Julia," Pa continued, seeing the worried look on his daughter's face. "Long as I'm around, no Cody has reason to fear."

It was true, Bill thought, watching his father with admiration. Pa had always taken care of them. He hadn't always stuck to one path. He had tried farming, politics, stagecoaching, trade, and now was back to farming again. But he always did what he set out to do, and he did it right. They might not be rich like the families of the river pilots, but Bill and his sisters had never wanted for anything. They followed their Pa's decisions without question, and he had never steered them wrong. Even when Pa had planned to take them out to California to join the gold rush, it was because he knew it was their best opportunity. And when folks in the wagon train took sick with cholera just before leaving, Pa wasn't shy about changing his mind back again and deciding they'd stay in Iowa.

Maybe most important, Bill thought, is that folks liked Pa. Wherever he went, folks seemed to take to him immediately. He had a way with people, he seemed to know how to talk to a person, an instinct for smoothing things over. He was a generous man and a good-hearted one. Bill felt a little swell of pride in his father. He was content to let Pa do the thinking for all of them. And if it took them over the prairie and into wild and unsettled new lands, all the better.

"My word, Mary, where did this butter come from?" Pa suddenly exclaimed.

Bill smiled to himself. The butter had been right in front of them all through lunch, and Pa had only just noticed it.

"Ma sealed up a jug of milk and tied it outside the wagon," said Eliza Alice with pride. "It bounced along beside us as we drove."

"And it churned itself!" said Ma with a smile. "Easiest pound of butter I ever made."

"If you aren't the cleverest thing, Mrs. Cody," said Pa. "But I've been saying that for I don't know how long, and it's always true."

Ma reached for his plate and filled it up again. It was only bread, cheese, and butter, but out in the fresh air it seemed as satisfying a feast as Bill had ever tasted.

"Have some more, Isaac," she said.

Bill lay back, using Turk's enormous body as a pillow, and peered up at the endless sky, patting his stomach and enjoying the satisfaction of security and abundance.

"We really shouldn't have come," said Julia anxiously. "Ma didn't want us to. Did you see her face, Bill?"

How could he have missed it? The brief smiles at lunchtime had been replaced by Ma's usual anxious expression, as Pa gave the children permission to go walking. Bill guiltily tried to erase Ma's worried looks from his mind. It was only a walk, for goodness' sake.

"Next year this time we'll be settled on our new farm, Julia," Bill said. "Maybe for a long time. We've got to explore while we can, don't you see? Anyway, we brought Nellie along, so you're still helping out, officially."

They had set out to walk to Big Creek, a half mile or so in the distance. Normally they packed up and were on their way as soon as the last bit of bread was eaten, but George had noticed a loose wheel on one of the wagons that needed tightening. Mary Hannah and Eliza Alice were napping on the blanket, and Ma and Martha were sitting in the shade of the wagon and doing some mending. Turk had fallen into a well-deserved sleep. When asked, Pa had given permission for the other children to walk ahead, with the promise that the wagons would catch up with them before long. It was the perfect opportunity to play Lewis and Clark, and they should have a good game even if Nellie did slow them up.

"You see, President Jefferson bought all this land," Julia was saying to Nellie as they arrived at Big Creek, "and they called it the Louisiana Territory. It was so much land that it took up more room than the whole rest of the United States, or what was the United States back then."

"And nobody knew what was in all that land," said Bill in a mysterious way. Nellie fixed her huge eyes on him. "What kind of Indians would they find there? Friendly ones . . . or not? What kind of wild animals? The territory was so big and wild, you couldn't ride across it in a whole month on your very best horse. So President Jefferson decided that somebody—" Here Bill paused for dramatic effect. "Somebody," he continued after a moment, "had to go and see what was there."

"So he sent Lewis and Clark," Julia cut in, "and they went up the Missouri River in a boat and saw things no American had ever seen before."

"And they had the most exciting and dangerous adventures any man ever did," Bill said with relish. "One of them at a place called Bad River. That's what we're playing."

This time Bill was to be Clark, and Julia was Lewis. Big Creek was to play the role of Bad River, and in the interests of peacekeeping, Nellie was granted the right to be Seaman, Lewis's black Newfoundland dog.

"Now we've just showed the three Teton Sioux chiefs our keelboat, and I'm going to escort them back to the riverbank in the canoe," Bill explained to Nellie and Julia.

"You'll stay in the keelboat with the men manning the swivel gun, Lewis," he continued. "But you keep a sharp eye on me. Remember, you're in the middle of the river, about seventy yards from shore. Watch me careful. As soon as the braves raise their bows at me, you shout for the men to steady their sights, and then you call out, 'Clark, are you in danger?' And I'll shout, 'Hold your fire.'"

"What do I say? What do I say?" said Nellie eagerly.

"You're keeping me safe in the boat, Nellie," said Julia.

"Seaman!" insisted Nellie.

"Seaman, then. You stay in the boat with me while Clark goes ashore."

"But what do I say?" Nellie asked.

"You don't say anything," said Bill, impatient to get on with the game. "Dogs can't talk."

Nellie's brown eyes brimmed with tears.

"I wanna say something," she wept. She might be only four, but Nellie knew how to make herself a pitiful sight when the situation required. Bill rolled his eyes at Julia, who was giving her little sister a hug.

"All right then, Ne—I mean, Seaman," said Julia. "After I shout 'Clark, are you in danger?' you bark 'Woof!' just as loud as you can."

"Woof!" shouted Nellie with gusto. Julia nodded with approval.

"Not bad," Bill said. "Not bad. Now let's start quick—or the wagons are going to get rolling and catch up with us before we get a chance to play."

Julia picked up Nellie and, with some difficulty, crossed from stone to stone over the rushing water until she reached the center of the creek, where there was a wide rock that they had agreed would represent Lewis's keelboat. Nellie crouched, doglike, at Julia's side. Bill began, with great ceremony, to escort the three Teton Sioux who had been his guests to the bank of the river. He moved with the strength of an explorer and the elegance of a diplomat. As he gestured to his three phantom companions, creating words and meaning with his hands, he felt himself slip fully into the role, and it seemed the whole landscape around him also transformed. The warm spring air gave way to the chill of a western autumn breeze. The burbling creek turned into the deep and dark Bad River. The watchful gaze of the Teton Sioux Indians, standing on the tree-lined bank of the river, made him tense with readiness. Bill relished this feeling, when time stood still and the world he knew blinked out and was replaced by one entirely of his own making. It was a feeling of complete power and wonder, and he never grew tired of it.

Bill stood alert and to attention, and as Julia watched him intently, she could practically see with her own eyes that the braves had whirled about and were leveling their bows at the head of Captain Clark.

"Clark, are you in danger?" Julia called, forgetting in her excitement to tell the men to steady their sights. Bill's line was next, but then Julia remembered the promise she'd made her little sister.

"Now, Nellie. Bark now."

There was no bark.

Julia reluctantly tore her eyes away from her brother and glanced to her side. There was no one else on the rock. Nellie was gone.

"Bill!" screamed Julia. The tone in her voice cut through Bill's imagined world like a knife, and one quick glance told him all he needed to know about what had happened.

They tore down the creek following the current—Julia on one side of the bank and Bill on the other. The water wasn't much more than two feet deep, but it moved quickly in some places.

"Nellie!" shouted Bill as he ran, and Julia echoed the call.

"Nellie!"

Bill had known this terror one time before. With his own eyes he had seen Sammy fly to the earth still clinging to the back of the horse—heard the sickening thud as his body connected with the ground. All the while knowing he should have tried harder to stop Sammy, should have warned him just how spooked Betsy really was. This was his fault, too, he thought, running as fast as he could but feeling like he was wading through molasses. He had persuaded Julia to come. He was Nellie's older brother. Her only brother. And he had failed her. He'd failed all the Codys.

Julia, running along the other bank, shouted her sister's name again and again. Her voice sounded a mile away.

Then Bill saw Nellie's shoe.

"Bill!" Julia cried. She had seen it, too, where it stuck out from a tangle of brush and branches that made a small dam in the creek.

Nellie's foot was visible, but the rest of her was covered over by the mass of branches in which she'd become entangled. Bill couldn't tell if her head was above water or not. She didn't seem to be kicking.

"Julia, help me lift it!" cried Bill, plunging into the creek. A small fallen tree lay on top of the tangle, its weight holding little Nellie down in the cold water.

Bill couldn't move it on his own, hard as he tried. Julia waded in and thrust her weight beneath the trunk, straining with all her might. Bill didn't feel it budge.

"I'm not strong enough," she sobbed. "I can't do it!"

"Julia, you've got to!" cried Bill. She tried again, weeping with the effort, but it was no use. Bill continued to shout encouragement at her. He had to make her strong, had to force it out of her. It was Nellie's only chance. Wading around to the center of the stream, close to Nellie's little shoe, Bill clawed and tore at the branches that held his sister down, all the while urging Julia to keep lifting. Then something made him glance up over the prairie, and he saw that the wagons were on the move. He could see Pa in front, driving a wagon, leading the trotting Orion alongside.

"Julia, it's Pa!" Bill cried. "Get his attention! Get him here quick!"

In a flash Julia leaped up the creek bank and jumped and waved frantically at her father. Her desperation was evident, and within seconds Pa had stopped the wagon and climbed onto Orion's back. He was at the creek in an instant, leaping out of the saddle before his horse had even slowed to a walk. The situation required no explanation.

Pa jumped into the water beside Bill. "On my

count, Bill, one two three!"

They lifted the trunk and then, while Pa held it up, Bill darted underneath, dragging Nellie free of the tangle. Bill staggered with her up the bank and laid her wet, still body on the warm grass. Pa was at her side immediately.

"Nellie-belle?" Pa said, shaking her gently. Her face looked slack and still, and reminded Bill horribly of the last time he'd seen Sammy, on his back with his eyes closed and the life running out of him. Pa rubbed his little daughter's arms, then turned her on her side and slapped her back. For a moment nothing happened. Then water ran out of Nellie's mouth, and in one miraculous moment she began to cough.

"That's right, sweetheart," Pa said. "Spit the water up. Spit it up, honey."

Nellie's closed eyes looked like tiny little burrows in her chalk-white face, but her chest rose and fell with steady breaths. Bill barely kept from sobbing with love and relief as he looked at his sister's dark curls pressed wetly over her small forehead.

"Nellie," he whispered, leaning over her. "Nellie-bellie, won't you say something?"

Nellie's eyes fluttered opened and stared blankly for a confused moment. Then they focused on Bill, and she opened her mouth.

"Woof," she said weakly.

"Oh, Nellie!" cried Bill, now crying in earnest, as Pa gathered her up into his arms.

In the distance Ma's carriage and George's wagon were growing closer. Ma seemed to be standing up in the carriage as she held the reins to get a better look at what was going on.

"What happened here?" Pa asked quickly.

"We were playing a game, sir," Bill said, looking his father straight in the eye. "And not watching Nellie as we promised. She must have fallen into the creek, and it swept her off before we knew what was happening. It was my idea and my game, and I take the blame for it."

Julia shook her head, but her tears were falling too rapidly and she couldn't find her voice.

Pa sat quietly for a minute, watching his three children. There were so many things Bill knew he could have said. There was responsibility and trust. There was family, and the already shared burden of loss. But Pa just watched the three of them, and as Ma's carriage drew closer, he said only one thing.

"Your ma is not to know about this, understand? Nellie was wading, and she slipped and fell in. That's all that happened here. Understand?"

They nodded.

Later that evening, as they unpacked their things at the farmhouse where they would lodge, Julia finally spoke to Bill.

"I shouldn't have been playing, Bill," she said. "I

should have stayed behind and kept Nellie with the wagons."

"Julia, it was my fault, mine alone," Bill said, barely able to look at her. He'd avoided her all afternoon, so ashamed was he of what he'd done. "You know that. I wonder that you can speak to me at all, after what almost happened."

"How can you say that?" cried Julia. "I was to look after Nellie. It was my responsibility!"

"I led you off," Bill said. "I persuaded—"

"Stop it!" Julia cried. "Stop protecting me, Bill. The truth of the matter is, if I'd been acting responsible as Ma wanted, if I'd been . . . if I'd been acting like a *girl*, none of this would have happened. I'd have sat watching Nellie and darning socks like Martha. Instead, I ran off to play with you, and I almost killed Nellie!"

Bill shook his head but said nothing. He knew the kind of guilt Julia was feeling. He felt it all the time.

"I may not be the kind of lady Martha is, but I've got to do better," Julia said quietly. "Much, much better."

Neither of them spoke anymore that night or mentioned the incident again.

Chapter Six

BUSHWHACKERS AND JAYHAWKERS

★ ★ ★

Had they really been traveling for three and a half weeks? Had it been only that long? Back in LeClaire Bill could never have imagined that a covered-wagon journey across two states might become routine. Some parts of it, though, had become as customary as his old Iowa chores. Up early, a quick breakfast, and the dash around to stow their belongings before getting under way—he did all these things practically without thinking.

And though he felt a little rush of pleasure each time he settled into Orion's saddle in the morning, it was no longer as exhilarating as it had been those first days out.

Bill still felt there was much to be said for a traveling life, but he was beginning to see the appeal of a permanent home, too. With luck and good weather, it shouldn't be too long in coming. Pa guessed they were now just a couple of days from Weston, where they would temporarily settle in with Uncle Elijah. Shifting in the saddle and stretching his tired muscles, Bill thought of this destination with pleasant anticipation.

They had gone for miles that day without coming to a lodging, and Ma had almost resigned herself to camping out for the night when they spotted a farmhouse in the distance. Pa didn't know any folks in this area of Missouri, but often farmers would lodge passing travelers for the night, and he hoped these people might be willing.

As they approached the house, Bill could see that it must belong to a family of some means. It was large and well kept, and there were a number of newly built outbuildings behind it. The bright-yellow clapboards looked freshly painted. Each window in the house had real glass panes, and the front door had a fancy storebought knob and knocker of brass. There were bushes and flowers lining the front walk—they seemed to have been planted there for no other reason than to make things look pretty.

Bill went with Pa to knock on the front door while Ma waited in the carriage with her daughters and Turk, who could be intimidating to strangers at first glance. The brass knocker made an impressive sound, and Bill began to feel uncomfortable as they waited.

"Don't you bet they got ice cream here, Pa?" he whispered. Ever since an old business partner of Pa's had served a dish of ice cream at dinner, Bill had developed a strange longing for it. He knew Ma wasn't likely to pay extra for this luxury, but Bill never gave up hope another creamy spoonful might find its way to his mouth. Before Pa could give his thoughts on the matter, the door opened.

A serving woman with graying blond hair and a crisp white apron looked at Pa without smiling.

"Yes?" she said, glancing over at Bill. Immediately he became aware of how dirty his face and clothes must be, after he'd been on the dusty roads all day.

"I wonder if I might speak with the master or missus of the house please, ma'am," said Pa. "My family and I are traveling to my brother's home in Weston, and we're looking for a place to put up for the night."

"Mrs. Burns is not in the habit of taking in lodgers," said the woman coldly, fixing her ice-blue eyes suspiciously on Bill.

"I'm sure she ain't, ma'am, but if I could have a word with her, I sure would appreciate it."

Bill knew why Pa wanted to ask face-to-face. People generally had a tough time saying no to his father when he asked something. Maybe it was his gentle rumbly voice, which was so calming to hear. Maybe it was his pleasant and honest eyes, and the way he had of looking right at a person like he could see them on the inside as well as out. Whatever it was, Pa usually got what he wanted. Even now, though clearly reluctant, the servant told them to wait as she closed the door in their faces.

Mrs. Burns appeared a moment later. She was an elegant woman, wearing a dress of deep-blue cashmere with a matching shawl that Bill knew Martha would ooh and aah over. She said nothing but looked at Pa expectantly. He introduced himself and explained his hope to lodge at her farm.

"Where are you traveling from?" she asked.

"LeClaire, Iowa, ma'am," Pa replied.

To Bill's surprise, the woman began to close the door.

"I'm afraid I can't help you," she said, but Pa quickly spoke.

"We're traveling to Weston to stay with my brother a spell," he said. "His name is Elijah Cody, ma'am. He's a respected citizen—maybe you've heard of him." They were only twenty or thirty miles from Weston now. It might be possible, Bill knew, for Mrs. Burns to have heard of his uncle.

"Elijah Cody?" said Mrs. Burns with some surprise. "But I know him well. My husband was Elijah's partner in the mercantile business for ten years until he died in fifty-two, Lord rest his soul. And my eldest son, Jim, often does business with him now. Your brother was here visiting not two weeks ago."

"Well, if that ain't something," said Pa with a chuckle.

"You certainly must stay, being Elijah's kin; there's no question about that," Mrs. Burns said. She was smiling now and acting more openly, but Bill still found her rather unappealing.

"Thank you kindly," Pa said. "There are eight of us Codys, ma'am, and a hired man with us, too, helping drive our teams. He's happy to bunk down anywhere as long as it's dry."

"A hired man?" Mrs. Burns asked, a shadow crossing her face.

"Yes, he's . . . well, there he is now," Pa said, pointing. George had climbed down from his wagon and was tending to the oxen. Mrs. Burns took a quick look at him and appeared satisfied. Bill wondered what little test George had just passed, and why Mrs. Burns's behavior seemed to go back and forth between cold and warm—well, maybe lukewarm.

"That'll be fine," she said. "Harriet will see you

all inside. You must be tired."

"You might say that, ma'am," Pa said with a smile. "Now get on, Bill. Go fetch your ma and sisters."

"Yes, sir," Bill said, and he trotted toward the family carriage. He had to laugh as he caught sight of them all sitting still in the coach. Ma and Martha were trying to look as if they hardly noticed Bill approaching when it was clear to him they were bursting with curiosity. He was pleased that the news he was bringing would make them happy—they would all enjoy spending the night in this fine house, even if he had been looking forward to sleeping under the stars for once.

"Ma, this lady knows Uncle Elijah, and she's asked us to stay overnight!" Bill said, and Ma's face brightened. To Bill she seemed happier since they had left LeClaire, more like her old self.

"What a lovely house," she said as Bill helped her down from the carriage.

"My word, isn't it just!" exclaimed Martha, handing Mary Hannah over to Julia. "Ma, I expect they'll have lovely china."

"And linens," added Eliza Alice, not quite sure if this was the right thing to say.

"And ice cream!" Bill said hopefully. Maybe it wouldn't be so bad staying here.

"What a treat," Ma said, as the girls stretched

their legs outside the carriage. "Overnighting in a lovely household such as this."

"Is my hair in place, Ma?" asked Martha.

"Have I any smudges on my face?" Julia asked.

Bill started to laugh, thinking Julia was making fun of Martha, but stopped himself when he saw his sister was serious.

"No, Julia," said Martha. "But let me smooth your hair a little."

The sight of Julia standing patiently while Martha fussed over her hair was more than Bill could stand. Ma had already started up toward the front door, with Mary Hannah in her arms and Eliza Alice in tow. As Martha bent down by the front of the carriage to straighten Nellie's dress and hair, Bill took Julia's elbow and pulled her several feet away.

"Some place, huh?" he whispered. "Come on, let's sneak off and explore some."

"You know I can't do that!" she whispered back angrily.

"Course you can!" Bill retorted. "We'll just slip off and—"

He broke off, astonished, as Julia simply pushed past him and joined Martha.

"I'm ready," Julia said to Martha, taking Nellie's hand. The three girls walked, in various states of primness, toward the house. Bill stared after Julia, his mouth slightly open. Was this what Julia had meant by trying harder? Could he not even ask her to take a walk anymore? He felt a little ball of resentment forming in his stomach. He had lost Sammy, and then Joe. Now it looked like he was going to lose Julia as well. It just wasn't fair. It was as plain and simple as that.

Still scowling, Bill whistled to Turk to follow him and walked out past the carriage, noticing the farmland spread out in all directions, like a rich green carpet.

"Who are you?" came a voice that was neither friendly nor unfriendly. Bill turned toward the sound. There was a boy nearby, with a shock of blond hair and sky-blue eyes. Bill was surprised. Mrs. Burns, to be honest, seemed too old to have a boy this age. He looked one, maybe two years older than Bill.

"My name's Bill Cody," he said. "I'm Elijah Cody's nephew. We're gonna be spending the night here at your ma's."

Bill noticed a slight change in the boy's face at the mention of Elijah's name—a slight softening. This certainly seemed a good place to be a Cody.

"She's my grandma," the boy corrected. "And you're a Cody. Well that's all right, then. My name's Matthew. My pa does work with your uncle, sometimes, in Weston."

"Hey," said Bill, feeling suddenly shy. With Julia

around, Bill had never felt too lonely, even though she wasn't a real boy. But since the trouble at Big Creek, he realized, she'd been less and less companionable, and it had never been more obvious than just this evening. Seeing Matthew made Bill see how much he missed the company of a boy his own age.

"That your dog?" Matthew asked, gesturing to Turk.

"Yep," Bill said with pride. "He's a mastiff. Strong as a mountain lion, and just as quick."

"He's tall enough," said Matthew, coming closer. "You could saddle him up and ride him in a pinch, I bet."

Bill laughed. "I just about tried a couple a times. Turk doesn't consider himself much civilized, though. He didn't take too well to the idea, and having plain sense, I respected his choice."

"Can I pet him?" Matthew asked, and Bill nodded.

"But you better let me introduce you proper," he added. "Easy now, Turk. This is Matthew, and he's okay. You let him live, boy."

Matthew gave a little laugh as he scratched the enormous dog's ears.

"I could use me a good dog," he said. "Last one I had run off."

"Turk is family," Bill said. "He won't run off 'less I do first."

"That carriage for your kin?" Matthew asked,

watching as George unharnessed Little Gray and Baker from Ma's rig.

Bill nodded. "My ma and pa," he said. "And five sisters."

Matthew looked horrified. "Five sisters?" he repeated. "Lord, you need yourself a whole army of dogs. I got two sisters myself, but both older'n me, thank heaven. They got themselves married off an' outta my hair, so it's all right."

It was nice to have someone understand. Joe had no sisters, and Bill always suspected he was a little sweet on Julia, anyway.

"Any brothers?" Bill asked. Matthew acted like he hadn't heard him and bent down to pat Turk again.

"Not now," he said finally, not looking up from the dog.

"Yeah. Me, too," Bill said.

Matthew caught his eye. "Yeah?"

"He was my older brother, Sammy. Twelve. Got himself into the saddle of a wild horse, and she bucked and landed on him."

"When was that?" asked Matthew.

"Five months back," said Bill. "Ma didn't want to stay home no more after that. So Pa wrote to Uncle Elijah, and we packed up our belongings and here we are."

Matthew nodded. "I had an older brother, too. Samuel. Same name. Funny, huh? He was eighteen;

this was a few years back. Got gold fever. Wanted to go out west so bad, he wouldn't hear talk of nothing else. Joined himself up with a party of men bent on prospecting and set out over the Oregon Trail with the wagon train. A few miles shy of Fort Bridger, half the group took sick with cholera. Samuel was one of the first to go. Don't even know where he's buried."

"That's rough," Bill said.

"Had a younger brother, too, called John. He wandered off picking berries one day and got himself drowned."

Bill thought of Nellie and suppressed a shudder.

"So now it's just me still home. I stay away as much as possible. Ma don't honestly care for me all that much—Johnny was always her favorite. So I travel with Pa on his business when I can. Other times just stay here with Grandma."

He said this matter-of-factly, without a trace of self-pity. Bill decided Matthew was all right. They could be friends, even. Seemed like maybe they could understand each other in ways other folks couldn't.

"So you been to Weston?" Bill asked.

"Sure. Live there some of the time. Pa keeps a place in town so he has somewhere to go when he's there."

Bill thought how rich a man would need to be to keep a whole house just to stay in sometimes.

"What's it like?"

"It's a lively town, I'll say that. First settler bought the land from an Indian trader for a barrel of whiskey, or so they say. Everyone comes to Weston sooner or later. As many as five boats at a time tyin' up at the dock, includin' all the biggest and fastest steamers. You got settlers and prospectors camping out on the banks of the river, buyin' provisions and waitin' their turn for the ferry to take 'em across the channel so they can get on out west. Dragoons come over from Fort Leavenworth to visit the saloons and let loose. Traders and merchants. Indians, sometimes. You name it, Weston's probably got it, and if she ain't, she don't want it."

"Sounds like a dream come true," said Bill, his imagination already taking flight with visions of men in buckskins or fancy army uniforms walking the streets as magnificent steamboats sailed by on the river.

"It ain't quiet, that's for sure. Your uncle has a place right in town, up on Main Street, and he's got a big farm, too, outside of town, like my pa. Raises hemp, mostly, and does himself a fine trade. My pa says your uncle Elijah's got the smartest head for doin' business of any man in these parts."

"That's what my pa says, too," said Bill proudly. "I ain't never met him myself."

"He reminds me of a teacher I once had," said

Matthew. "All serious and proper. But he's regular people, too, I guess. Even taught me a thing or two that's useful. One summer me and John made a fair living buying apples for twenty-five cents a peck and sellin' 'em across the river at Fort Leavenworth. We got so much for 'em that even after the ten-cent round-trip ferry ticket, we still made a good sixty cents on top of what we put in. It was your uncle's idea, and I 'preciated it. He don't smile much, though."

It didn't sound like living with Uncle Elijah would be too lively, but Bill thought Weston itself would certainly make up for whatever his uncle might lack in fun.

"You wanna play something?" asked Matthew.

"Sure," said Bill.

"We could play ball, or race. I got a set of marbles. There's not all that much to do around here. Sometimes," he continued, a little self-consciously, "I just go out scouting, you know. . . ." His voice trailed off.

"I do that, too," Bill said excitely. " 'Cept I got in trouble last time, playing Lewis and Clark instead of watching my sister. She almost—she got soaking wet in the creek."

Matthew's eyes lit up.

"Well, ain't none of your sisters around right now."

"You want to pretend we're explorers?" Bill asked, glad all of a sudden Julia wasn't there.

"I got a better game," said Matthew. "Let's play bushwhackers and jayhawkers."

"Fine by me." Bill was unfamiliar with those words but not willing to admit it to Matthew.

"I'll be the bushwhacker, and you be the jayhawker. You can be riding in your wagon, and I'll be waiting to ambush you. I gotta ask one of the questions, and you won't know how to answer it right."

"One of the questions?" asked Bill, growing more confused.

"Yeah, I gotta ask 'Are you sound on the goose?' and 'Are you all right on the hemp?' And when you don't know how to answer, I'll know I got me a jayhawker. And then we fight."

It was as clear as a blizzard at midnight. Bill had no idea what Matthew was talking about, but he hoped he could bluff his way along.

"Okay," said Bill.

They walked down past one of the well-kept barns to where a wooded thicket began. Matthew made a great spectacle of concealing himself by climbing right into the center of a fat bush and hunching down inside it. It was a bit showy for Bill's taste, but for all his confusion he was beginning to enjoy himself. He drew himself up as an unsuspecting traveler and headed toward the spot where

Matthew was hidden away, an island of little trees and bushes. Bill imagined it into a proper forest and himself into a settler, heading west to start a new life. He was really beginning to enjoy himself. This was just the sort of game he might be playing with Joe at this very moment, if he'd still been back in Iowa.

As Bill passed by the fat bush, Matthew leaped out and blocked his path.

"You there," Matthew said sternly. "Where do you hail from, and what's your business in these parts?"

"I'm moving west with my family," Bill said, gesturing to the occupants of his imaginary wagon train. "We're traveling from Iowa."

"Iowa?" shouted Matthew, looking enraged. "Are you sound on the goose?"

"Sound on the ground at the moment, if you please," Bill retorted. It seemed a clever way to avoid admitting that he didn't understand the question.

"Answer me, you scoundrel. Are you all right on the hemp?"

"I don't know what in tarnation you're talking about," Bill said truthfully.

"I knew it!" Matthew yelled triumphantly. "I got me a jayhawker. Get down off that wagon, you scoundrel. I'll give you a thrashing you won't never recover from. Get down here, you blue-belly! You pesthouse pauper, I'll getcha! Come on and face me like a man, you mud sill!"

Though he hadn't heard most of these words before, Bill knew when he was being insulted. He placed himself in front of Matthew and drew out the sharpest and most wickedly long knife his imagination could conjure.

"Well, here I am, then," Bill cried. "I ain't afraid of you or nobody else!"

"I can take you in my sleep!" Matthew shouted, fairly hopping up and down in his manufactured rage. His face had turned red. "I'll cut your throat where you stand and send your body back east, you rotten Free-Soiler. I'll hang every one of you white-livered abolitionists till the last breath is choked outa you."

Free-Soiler? Abolitionist?

"Wait a second," said Bill suddenly. "Matthew, what exactly are we doing?"

Matthew looked at Bill like he had two heads, but before he could answer, Bill heard the sound of his ma's voice calling from the back porch. Of course. It had begun to get dark, and Ma was beginning to worry.

"That's my ma calling," Bill said. It was plenty irritating, but Bill had to admit to himself that he was also a little relieved at the interruption. Bill heard the sound of another voice, this one belonging to Mrs. Burns.

"You boys get yourselves inside and wash up,"

Mrs. Burns called. "It's nearly suppertime. I mean right now. Matthew Burns, you hear me?"

"Coming!" called Matthew. "We better go quick," he added, suddenly a placid and normal-looking boy once again. "I'm starved."

Bill followed him to the house, his unanswered question weighing heavily on his mind.

"Thank you so much, Mrs. Burns," Ma said. "I don't know that I've ever had finer food or seen a more beautifully laid table."

They were eating the last of their preserved peaches, which to Bill's astonishment had indeed been served with ice cream. The maid, Harriet, was now pouring steaming cups of coffee for the grown-ups from an elegant silver pot.

Bill had been unusually quiet throughout supper, but the food and tableware were distraction enough, and no one seemed to think anything was amiss. Bill himself was much less excited than he should have been. Not even the sweet, cold spoonfuls, creamy and rich, could rouse him from his mood. He watched Matthew cram a large peach slice into his mouth. He'd watched him all through dinner, trying to figure him out.

"We'll be living with Elijah until we stake our claim," Pa was saying.

"Seek his advice, and see that you heed it," Mrs.

Burns said. "Elijah will know what's best. He'll know where the trouble spots are, and which settlers would be . . . inappropriate as neighbors."

Bill didn't like the tone of her voice. It sounded like she was giving orders to Pa. But Pa didn't seem to mind.

"Trouble spots?" he said with a laugh. "As I understand it, ma'am, there's no one on that land now but soldiers and Indians. I don't suppose I'd be finding much in the way of trouble, even if I went out looking for it."

"With all due respect, Mr. Cody, you couldn't be more wrong," said Mrs. Burns. "But this is hardly proper supper conversation."

"I've never seen finer china," Ma said quickly. "Tell me, Mrs. Burns, how did you come by it?"

The rest of the supper hour was devoted to a detailed discussion of the pedigree of each plate, fork, and goblet and the origins of the linens and lace tablecloths. Bill was truly thankful when the lateness of the hour was discovered, and he quickly accepted the suggestion that he and his sisters get themselves ready for bed.

Mrs. Burns's house had two guest rooms, in addition to her room, Matthew's room, and his pa's. Bill thought a house with five bedrooms was pretty fine. Back in LeClaire, they had had only three bedrooms all together, and the one Bill had shared with Sammy was tiny, little more than a broom closet. And the dining room—that was something else. Mrs. Burns had a whole separate room just for eating, instead of taking meals in the kitchen as the Codys always had. Off the dining room was another room Mrs. Burns called the parlor, and that was a room just for sitting in, and maybe taking a cup of tea and popping some corn. Rooms for eating, and rooms for sitting, when the kitchen would do perfectly well for both! Bill knew the river pilots' grand houses back in LeClaire had these special rooms, too, but everyone knew steamer pilots weren't regular people. To see an everyday-seeming person like Mrs. Burns surrounded by all this luxury made Bill wonder.

Ma, Pa, and Mary Hannah would take one of the guest rooms, and the older girls the other. Bill would sleep in Matthew's room, but he would have a bed to himself. The trundle slid out neatly from below Matthew's bed, looking plump and warm beneath the quilt and blankets.

Matthew was eager to play some more, and said if they pled loudly enough, they might be allowed to stay up an additional hour. Bill begged off as politely as possible. They would be leaving early in the morning, he explained, and there was nothing worse than a full day in the saddle when you hadn't slept enough the night before. He didn't bring up bushwhackers and jayhawkers. By now,

Bill wasn't sure he wanted to explore this subject with Matthew. He was sure he didn't want to play the game again, though.

As he snuggled under the covers, he barely noticed the mattress and pillows, which were filled with real feather down rather than hay, like every other bed he'd ever slept in. It was like lying down in a cloud, but it gave him no comfort. In spite of what he'd told Matthew, he was wide-awake, and his mind was racing.

Matthew's sleeping form was illuminated by moonlight shining through the window. With his quiet breathing and shock of blond hair, he looked almost angelic in the silver light. But Bill kept seeing their game, and the gleeful rage with which Matthew had attacked the imaginary abolitionist. He thought back to Harriet's and Mrs. Burns's odd manner when they had first greeted the Codys. Being from Iowa seemed to be an issue with them. Iowa was a free state. Did that have something to do with it? If only Sammy were here, he thought. They could talk it over together, figure it out. But of course, Sammy wasn't here.

Bill's thoughts were disturbing. For the first time in his life, Bill found himself wondering if Pa was right—if this slavery question really had so little to do with them. If it really could be avoided, as Pa said, by intent alone.

CHAPTER SEVEN
WESTON

★ ★ ★

Bill didn't know where to look first. There was so much going on, so many competing sounds and smells, that he could scarcely focus on one thing for fear of missing another.

They had arrived in Weston soon after the land arched itself into rolling hills and bluffs. It was only two days' travel from the Burns farm, but it seemed like another world

entirely. The town lay like a hidden treasure nestled into the swelling landscape. A church spire towered over the buildings that spread themselves out in brick and timber all the way down to the wharf. Beyond the several main streets the houses were farther apart, and the land gradually relaxed into sprawling farms in the distance. Trees of various shapes and sizes dotted the countryside. The Missouri River herself poked in toward the town, creating a natural bay where steamers and ferries could load and unload their cargo.

Pa halted their little wagon train outside a dry goods store on Main Street. He went inside to ask the whereabouts of Elijah's house, only agreeing to leave the wagons after Bill earnestly promised not to wander.

It was frustrating, but at least atop Orion he could see a considerable amount of the town. The streets fairly seethed with humanity. Men and women poured in and out of the various shops—wheelwrights', dry goods stores, and bakeries. LeClaire had always seemed big and busy enough to Bill, but compared to this it was nothing. A variety of smells mingled and competed in the air—baked goods, smelting iron, and stable smells, to name just a few. Teams of horses and oxen were led back and forth as their owners negotiated their sale with interested travelers. Men rode by on horseback with bulging carpetbags and other parcels strapped to the backs of their saddles, or flung over their horses' hindquarters. If only Sammy could see this, Bill thought wistfully. It would all be perfect, if only Sammy were here.

Bill looked down the length of Main Street to where the river met the bottom of the hill. He could see two large steamers preparing to tie up at the docks. As the ropes were uncoiled, the bigger of the two boats opened up her whistle and sounded a shrill call. Moments later, like an answer, a bell in the gold-topped steeple of a surrounding church pealed loudly. Immediately the doors of nearby stores and saloons opened up, and groups of men rushed down to the river, jostling and pushing one another in a way that seemed more serious than good-natured.

Bill knew that the arrival of any steamer required the services of stevedores to unload the cargo and draymen to load the cargo onto their flat wagons and deliver it to merchants. Apparently there was such a surplus of these men in Weston that they had to shove one another out of the way to get the work. It certainly seemed to be an event—all over town men and women drifted toward the wharves to watch the goings-on.

Bill itched to join them. He was practically frantic to explore the wharf and to investigate the tents that had been erected up and down the riverbanks, probably by settlers waiting for a ferry. It was agony to be in full view of those two magnificent steamers and not get close enough to learn their names. Surely it would be all right to nudge Orion forward just a bit, to get just a little farther down the street. Even fifteen or twenty feet would be a help. But temptation fled in the face of Pa, who was coming out of the store with a merchant and nodding as the man pointed toward the top of Main Street, away from the river.

"Much obliged, sir," Pa said, then hurried over to the carriage where Ma and the girls were patiently waiting. Bill, unable to sit still another moment, walked Orion in small circles.

"We're going to turn 'em around, George," Pa called over his shoulder. "I'll take my team, and you lead Mary's around first, then see to your own."

"How far is it, Pa?" Bill asked. He knew he shouldn't ask, that he should be patient, but it was suddenly the most important thing in the world to know how long it would be until he saw where, in this bustling town, he would be staying.

"We're practically there, son," said Pa. "Two streets up, corner of Short and Main."

And indeed, they arrived in just a few minutes. Bill looked eagerly at his uncle's house. It was a solid two-story frame building sporting a fresh coat of white paint. It wasn't as large or as elegant as the Burnses' farmhouse, but to Bill it looked pretty handsome for a town building, and from the size of it, he guessed it had a dining room and a parlor, too.

Still, as the wagons came to a stop in front of the building, Bill felt a little disappointed that the moment seemed so ordinary. For almost a month they had devoted each day to getting to this place. And though they had not been threatened by storms, Indians, or sudden illness the way the California gold seekers were, it had still been an exhausting journey. After all their talk of reaching Weston, after all the anticipation, it seemed a bit of a letdown to suddenly arrive at Uncle Elijah's door-step with no fanfare.

As Bill mulled these thoughts over in his mind, the front door opened and a tall, dark-haired man came out.

"Is that Isaac?" the man called, and Pa leaped off his wagon.

"Elijah! It's been a long spell," Pa said, and the two men shared a brief embrace that seemed more respectful than affectionate. Of course, Bill remembered, the brothers had not seen each other since just before Pa married Ma, over thirteen years ago.

"Good to see you here safely," said Uncle Elijah. "How did the family fare?"

"Slightly the worse for wear," Ma said, taking the hand Uncle Elijah offered and climbing out of the carriage with a smile. "But in good health and thankful for your hospitality, Elijah."

"Glad to hear it," Uncle Elijah said. "It's been too long, Mary. And my goodness, is this Martha? You were just a tiny thing when I last saw you, child—the day Kit Carson came to town. I don't expect you remember that, though."

"I remember it completely," Martha said, glancing up at the white house and then at her uncle with a look of satisfaction. "He was an altogether memorable man."

Even the sound of his hero's name couldn't distract Bill from watching his uncle greet the family. So much depended on Uncle Elijah, Bill realized suddenly. Pa would be relying on him in many ways, especially on how to go about staking their claim in Kansas Territory. What if Uncle Elijah decided he didn't like them? What if he decided he didn't like Bill? Bill felt frozen on top of Orion.

"Julia, you are the spitting image of your mother," Uncle Elijah was saying. He had obviously paid close attention to the letters Ma and Pa had sent over the years. He knew everyone's name without hesitation. "And Eliza Alice, there's a little girl just your age living next door. Her pa's a friend of mine."

Eliza Alice gave a cry of delight, then immediately flushed. Little girls should be quiet and restrained.

"And these are my youngest," Ma said. "Nellie

and Mary Hannah. But where's Bill?"

"I'm right here, Ma," Bill said. His voice sounded feeble to his ears.

"Goodness gracious, Bill, get down off that horse and meet your uncle."

"My man will see to your mount, son," said Elijah, fixing his brown eyes on Bill.

Now Bill dismounted, embarassed to seem lacking in manners, and turned to face his uncle. Uncle Elijah was taller than Pa, and darker, too, in the hair and eyes. He had the look of a smart man, and one not to be trifled with. His store-bought clothes and gold watch chain indicated his wealth. He smiled at Bill when they shook hands, but Bill noticed the smile didn't quite take around the eyes.

"Pleased to meet you, sir," said Bill loudly, drawing himself up to his full height. "I heard many fine things about you, specially at the Burns place."

"Ellen Burns?" asked Uncle Elijah in surprise, addressing the question to Pa.

"The same," Pa replied. "'Twas quite a coincidence. We happened by her farmhouse looking for lodgings two nights ago."

"They're good people," Uncle Elijah said in a somber way. "A shame, losing Julian so suddenly. He was a sharp businessman. But let's get out of the street before the drays run us down."

Looking down at the river, Bill could see that

the flat wagons had now been loaded high with cargo, and the draymen were preparing their teams of oxen to haul the drays up Main Street.

"Come along," Uncle Elijah said, a little impatiently, as the family watched the sight. "My men will see to your teams."

Bill went inside last. With a feeling of regret, he stepped off the noisy and busy street and into his uncle's house, which seemed dark and quiet in comparison.

Pa and Uncle Elijah talked late into the night. At first Bill was too interested in the noises coming from the street to pay attention to their conversation. Unlike LeClaire, Weston was as lively after sundown as it had been after noon, and Bill lay in bed fascinated by the sounds of men and horses floating through his window, the little waves of music and footfalls that wafted in and out of earshot like dreams. But after a time, little snippets of conversation from the parlor reached his ears. Uncle Elijah must have left the window by the sofa open, and the sound of their voices drifted into the room where Bill was. He wanted to hear what they were saying, but even hanging out the window, he could not quite make out their words. So he did a bad thing.

It wasn't that Bill thought his pa was trying to hide anything from him. But grown-ups spoke more freely without children around—that was simply a fact. Bill was sure that his uncle and Pa were talking about the claim, and about the political situation in these parts, and he wanted to hear for himself what Uncle Elijah had to say. Since spending the night with Matthew two days earlier, he hadn't been able to shake a nagging fear that Pa was being too optimistic, and eavesdropping seemed the only way at the moment to get any more information.

Though he knew he would be in fearful trouble if caught, Bill slipped his britches and boots on and lowered himself carefully out the window, thankful his room faced the backyard. Once on the ground, he stole like a horse thief around the side of the house. Sammy would do the same if he were here, he thought to himself, creeping to the open parlor windows. There, he seated himself on the ground. Immediately he could hear their conversation as clearly as if he were right in the room.

"What about the Indian situation?" Pa was saying. "As I understand it, most of the local tribes have been moved at least once already. They were told the Kansas and Nebraska territories would be theirs forever, and now the government is moving them again. Sounds like trouble to me."

"I don't think so," came Uncle Elijah's voice, which was deeper than Pa's. "Things have been moving along peaceably so far. Word from Fort Leavenworth is the government is more concerned about finding a faster and safer route to California than any Indian troubles, least this far east.

"Now I can set you up with some goods if you want to try your hand at trading some," Uncle Elijah continued. "But there's an established trading post already in the area, and Rively runs a sharp and lively business. You'll have to be competitive, provide things he can't get or doesn't know folks want."

"I was thinking of starting with some of the locals," Pa said. "Maybe the Kickapoo you told me about."

"Well, I can make some introductions," Uncle Elijah said in his crisp way. Bill had noticed his uncle didn't speak the same way Pa did. Uncle Elijah got around words differently. More carefully, like a schoolteacher. "But make sure Rively knows what you're doing. Make a point of introducing yourself. He'll see things differently if it doesn't seem like you're trying to pull the wool over his eyes."

"I'll take care of it," Pa said. "It's not as if I want to run the man out of business. Just looking to do a little trading while our claim gets settled and we get to building our new place."

"And you've got to remember, Isaac, that Rively and his men are proslavers."

"Don't make no difference to me what they are," Pa said, and Uncle Elijah made an exasperated noise.

"Isaac, I'm here to tell you that you're reading this thing wrong. I got the feeling from your letters you figured you could just keep quiet about all this, but I'm telling you it isn't so. Senator Atchison is breathing fire down our necks, practically ordering our boys to get themselves over to Kansas and squash the Free-Soilers by any means necessary. It isn't enough to keep quiet about it. You've got to tell people what they want to hear, and most folks hereabouts want to know that you're sound on the goose."

Bill almost exclaimed in surprise as he recognized the expression Matthew had used during their game. To be sound on the goose means you're proslavery, Bill thought. Probably so did being all right on the hemp. It all made more sense now.

"Are you suggesting that I lie?" Pa said.

"Yes, Isaac, I am," said Uncle Elijah bluntly. There was a shocked silence. Bill wondered what Pa would say to this. He knew his father couldn't abide dishonesty of any kind. It was the main reason he'd gotten out of politics practically as soon as he'd gotten in.

"Elijah," said Pa finally, "I've always known you to be a good man and an upstanding citizen. But what you're saying here—"

"I am both those things," Uncle Elijah interrupted, "and something more, too. I'm an active participant in this community. I not only hear the gossip, I hear the facts. I'm respected here."

"And you're a slaveholder," Pa said. Bill clamped his hand over his mouth to prevent himself from exclaiming out loud. It hadn't occurred to him to think about it before, but he guessed it made sense. Missouri was a slave state, and Uncle Elijah raised crops. But Bill had never met a slaveholder before, let alone a slave. He realized now that Mrs. Burns probably had slaves, too.

"Well, of course I have slaves, Isaac," Uncle Elijah said calmly. "It's not exactly a secret. I'm a Missouri hemp farmer. You can't raise that crop without a great deal of labor."

"And what position do you take on this whole business?" Pa pressed.

"Same as I recommend to you. I take no active part in any organizations, but most everyone in these parts is proslavery, and I let them believe I am, too."

"But you're not," Pa said. The statement had a question in it, Bill noticed.

"That's not something I'm generally willing to admit," Uncle Elijah said. "And anyhow, it depends on how you look at it. Between you and me, yes. I'd just as soon see slavery restricted. But so long as it's legal in Missouri, I intend to profit from it.

There isn't a man in this state who can claim to treat his slaves better than I do, and if the whole business is outlawed, I'll happily see them on their way or hire them on as paid labor. But until that day, I'll hold my tongue and not go against the system. And if you value your family and your livelihood, you'll do the same."

"I'm happy to not let people know where I stand on the issue. It's what I'm planning to do anyway. But do you really expect," Pa said angrily, "that if some group of proslavery men *asks* me where I stand, I can brew up some story about how I'm with them all the way, and to hell and damnation with the abolitionists? You talk about valuing my family, Elijah. How can I lie to the world, then expect my family to respect me?"

"There are other things you can do, to avoid outright deception," Uncle Elijah said. "Nod when other men are talking. Avoid fraternizing with known Free-Soilers. Give the appearance of sympathy to the proslavers. Steer clear of situations where the question is going to be put point-blank to you."

"It's still a lie," Pa said.

Uncle Elijah made an explosive noise of irritation.

"You just don't get it, do you, Isaac?" he cried. "These are troubling times, and the worst is yet to come! What does honesty matter when your life and livelihood are at stake? I've got a wife and child in our farmhouse outside of town. I have a responsibility to them. If I started making trouble on this issue, people could get it in their heads to take it out on them!" He paused, and when he started speaking again, his voice was calmer. "A man's got to do whatever is necessary to keep himself and his family out of it. And I'm family, too, Isaac. People won't be so quick to ask questions about you because you're my brother, and my name means something in this town. But believe me, they'll be watching you. What you say, what you do while in Weston, affects me. Remember whose hospitality is keeping you here."

There was a long silence.

"So you're saying," Pa said, "that as long as I'm staying under your roof, I must pretend to sympathize with your slaveholding friends and make no trouble."

Something had come into Pa's voice, something hard, that worried Bill.

"I am urging you to do so at *all* times," Uncle Elijah said gently. "But yes, Isaac. While you are in my house, I must insist that you call no undue attention to yourself."

"Very well then," said Pa, his voice still strange. There was a pause, and then he added, "It's getting late."

Bill heard the sound of a chair being scraped back.

"The bill opening up Kansas Territory has passed in the House now," Uncle Elijah said. "All that's needed to make it official is for President Pierce to sign it. It could be days, maybe weeks, until we hear. Your family might be more comfortable at the farm-house with Louisa."

"You're probably right," said Pa. "We can move on out there tomorrow."

"And I suggest you get yourself across the river as soon as possible. Lots of folks got the same idea as you, getting here early to be ready to claim land the second that bill is law. You're going to want to have your claim picked out, and some kind of structure built there to show others the land is taken. I know the land well, and there's a pretty piece in Salt Creek Valley I think you ought to have a look at. The land will be easy to clear, but there are trees close by for timber, and it's just a few miles from the fort. If you can get there and nobody has beaten you to it, mark it out. And once you've done that, it would be best for you to stay there, to keep claim jumpers away."

"I thought it wasn't legal to stake a claim till the law took effect," Pa said, sounding tired.

"There's ways around the law, and you'll need to take them if you want a decent piece of land. What's important is to be there, and ready, so it's just a matter of paperwork once the bill is signed. I know the quartermaster at Fort Leavenworth, and I've told him to meet with you, as a personal favor. See if he can get the Indian agent's okay for you to graze some horses on the land. If he likes you, he might even give you a contract to provide the fort with some hay. Take anything he offers you. Any official sanction you got puts you ahead of the other squatters and claim jumpers."

"All right," Pa said. "I can go tomorrow morning, if you'll help Mary get to the farmhouse."

"I'm happy to come along, show you the land myself."

"Thanks just the same, but I'll be fine on my own," Pa said. "You don't need to worry," he added. "My word is good. Long as we're staying with you, I'll play this game your way."

"I know you will, Isaac," Uncle Elijah said. "I'm not doubting you. I just thought you might be able to use some help in Kansas. I know the land, after all."

"I'll do it on my own, just the same. Maybe I'll take Bill along. Show him the fort. He ain't never even seen a dragoon or an Indian before, for all his imagining. Yes, that'll do. I'll head for the Kansas Territory in the morning, and bring the boy along."

Still crouched, frozen beneath the window, Bill should have felt happy. Exultant. He'd always wanted to visit a real live fort and see dragoons.

But Uncle Elijah's strong words of caution rang in his ears. Because in spite of everything he knew about his father, in spite of trusting him and loving him, Bill couldn't help but feel that Uncle Elijah could be right. That they might be in trouble here. That things might become ugly for his family if they weren't careful.

He crept back around the house and into his room, but it was many hours before he slept.

CHAPTER EIGHT

KANSAS TERRITORY

★ ★ ★

Folks could spend days by the river, in line for a place on the ferry, especially if they had a prairie schooner and a team of oxen to transport. Some creeks and rivers could simply be forded on foot, but not the Missouri. Its currents and channels were too unpredictable. Going any way other than by boat just wasn't safe. Up and down the Missouri, every town that ran ferries was crowded with people waiting for passage. But Bill and his father had only their two horses and three small saddle-bags of supplies. And the name Elijah Cody went a long way in these parts, Bill was learning. Uncle Elijah knew a man named Wells in Rialto, just a mile downriver from Weston, who had started up a new ferry service making trips to Fort Leavenworth. Wells had purchased a brand-new steam ferryboat, and early in the morning Uncle Elijah escorted Pa and Bill to Rialto and had no trouble getting them a place on the very next ferry to the fort.

Bill wouldn't have minded a longer wait. All the activity on the riverfront in Rialto was fascinating to watch. Just as in Weston, tents and campsites lined the riverbanks, occupied by settlers and gold seekers waiting for the ferry. Spring was the height of the busy time for westwarders, and the anticipated opening of Kansas Territory had greatly increased the demand for ferries. For all but the wealthiest of travelers, who could bribe their way on, or those who traveled light, there was nothing to do but pitch a tent near the river and wait.

The ferryman's call came all too quickly, and it was only Pa's reminder of the sights awaiting them in Fort Leavenworth that consoled Bill.

As near as Bill could reckon, there were close to three hundred people on the ferry. The lower deck was tightly packed with horses and mules, and the upper decks held the wagons and people, most of them men. The mood was merry and raucous, and Bill felt as if he had stumbled into a giant floating saloon. Everywhere there were small groups of men playing cards or drinking, though it was not even nine in the morning. Some had gotten out their fiddles and were playing lively tunes in competition with one another. Everywhere there were little pockets of families, and Bill noticed the mothers keeping tight hold of their children. Ma and Martha would be in a state when their turn came to make the crossing, he thought with some amusement.

The fort lay downriver on the west side of the Missouri, just five or six miles from Rialto and Weston, and once the paddlewheel began to turn and the ferry got moving, the trip wasn't more than an hour. Bill could barely tell he was on the water, so smooth was the ferry, and he couldn't help feeling a little cheated somehow. As the ferry approached the fort, though, he felt his excitement building. He elbowed his way to the railing, and from his position up on the ferry's top level, he had a good view of the fort. Just beyond the landing, the ground rose steeply behind a three-story wooden structure Pa said was the quartermaster's storehouse. A dirt path led past the storehouse about a quarter of a mile up the hill to a grassy quadrangle surrounded by buildings. It looked more like a village than a fort—beyond this cluster of buildings were a number of handsome houses that Pa guessed were the homes of officers. A grove of elm trees stood behind the quadrangle, and the landscape in the distance was hilly and lush, speckled with trees and streams.

After what seemed like an eternity, the ferryman let down the gangplank and began unloading passengers. They collected the horses, and following his father, Bill led Orion carefully down the gangplank. At the bottom Bill placed both feet firmly on the ground. He was now in Kansas Territory.

Pa wanted to introduce himself to the quartermaster right away and request permission to graze his horses as Elijah had suggested. Pa explained Uncle Elijah's plan to Bill—how permission to graze horses and receipt of a contract to put up hay at the fort might lead to authorization to build a temporary structure on the land, all-important steps in establishing a presence on the land before staking a claim. Bill had to keep reminding himself that he wasn't supposed to have heard any of this before, and he nodded frequently as Pa explained Elijah's thinking.

While Pa went into the storehouse to search for the quartermaster, Bill wandered up the hill and led Orion and Pa's mount, Little Gray, toward the rectangular grassy area the ferryman had referred to as the Main Parade. Surrounded by buildings and stables, the area was aptly named, for, as Bill approached, he could see that a company of dragoons was proudly completing a full-dress parade.

The sight took Bill's breath away. He had read newspaper articles about the dragoons, but had never seen these hearty cavalrymen and their magnificent horses. It was Colonel Kearney's company of dragoons, once stationed at this very fort, that had required the services of Kit Carson on their California expedition during the Mexican War.

Bill could hardly take his eyes off the razor-straight columns of mounted soldiers in their light-blue pants and jackets of dark-blue wool and gold trim. Their Mississippi rifles and sabers gleamed in the sunlight, and their navy-blue hats, with the company letters emblazoned in brass, were the finest he'd ever seen. The way Orion and Little Gray were watching the proceedings, it seemed to Bill that they felt the same admiration that he felt himself.

Off to one side, the company captain was shouting out commands like "Form line!" and "Wheel left!" Though he'd never actually seen a drill before, Bill didn't need anyone to explain what was going on. The men were practicing going from one formation to another. Each man was on horseback, and Bill knew that every horse would naturally want to trot at its own speed. The men had to practice their formations so that all the horses moved at exactly the same time. Bill had read enough about the dragoons' experience in the Mexican War to understand that they had to be able to go from columns of three or four abreast to several straight lines quickly and with absolute precision. If they ran into the enemy while traveling in columns, they had to be ready to fight almost instantly. The drill went on for ages, but Bill never grew bored watching the men guide their horses with seemingly no effort, or dismount and drop to their knees, loading their guns.

When the drill finally ended and the dragoons rode off, Bill let out a deep breath. It had been perfect.

He now looked around the fort.

Several frontiersmen in faded buckskin shirts and britches stood idly watching the activities. Private carriages gathered by the barracks in front of the quadrangle, carrying wealthy sightseers from Missouri who wished to glimpse the famous dragoons in action. Off to the side, several lean, dark figures caught Bill's eye. As he studied them from a distance, he wondered at their strange mix of beads, buckskin, and feathers. Indians, he realized all at once, almost rigid with astonishment. He'd never seen Indians before.

It was all too much to take in. Braves, trappers, and mountain men. Mounted dragoons cantering across the Main Parade. The well-to-do sightseers. Here it seemed that every kind of person in the world had a representative, all wandering casually around. Still, Bill found his eye kept returning to the buckskin-clad frontiersmen. These men, sought out as scouts by the fort, most appealed to Bill. The best of them, men like Kit Carson and Jim Bridger, were involved in just about everything big and important going on. But they were still their own men, beholden to none.

"You look like you swallowed a prairie dog, son," came Pa's amused voice.

Bill couldn't manage to find his voice, and Pa laughed.

"I know," he said. "There's a bit of everything here, and you ain't seen none of it before. Don't worry, Bill. There'll be plenty of time for you to soak it all up. But right now we got to get moving. I did real well with the quartermaster—he's agreed to let me graze some horses and put up some hay for the fort, over Government Hill in Salt Creek Valley. There's a piece of land there Elijah wants us to take a look at. Says it might make a pretty claim if no settlers are on the land yet. We'll set up camp there, and maybe do some trading."

Bill silently pulled himself away from the Main Parade. He'd seen enough to last him for days, he thought. He climbed into the saddle and nudged Orion gently. The horse followed Pa and Little Gray away from the fort and into the hilly and wooded landscape beyond. Gradually the many noises from the fort faded away.

Father and son climbed a hill on their horses. The air was crisp and clear, and the only sound was the hoofbeats of their horses and the crackling of brush and dried leaves. When he closed his eyes, Bill pretended he was the first American ever to ascend this path. He imagined how Lewis and Clark must have felt as they pushed upward against the currents of the Missouri River, into the great unknown.

"Have yourself a look, Bill," Pa said. Bill opened his eyes and gasped with pleasure.

They had reached the very top of the hill, and spread out below them in the distance was a splendid and lush valley that stretched as far as Bill could see. The trees, brush, and wildflowers were in the full splendor of their spring youth, and the small rivers and streams that snaked through the countryside shone blue as the sky. It was rich land, that was for certain. A family could make a good home there.

Even more amazing, though, were the hundreds upon hundreds of covered wagons lining the rivers and tributaries below. They dominated the countryside like a vast herd of white grazing animals.

"Who are they?" asked the astonished Bill. "Where are they all going?"

"Emigrants, mostly," Pa replied. "That and freighters. The emigrants are folks heading out west to California or Oregon. I hear those parts are a paradise to behold, if you can survive the trip out there. And there's still men striking gold and getting rich. Then there's parties of Mormons bound for Salt Lake. Quartermaster warned me to steer clear of them. They lost thirty so far to cholera, and more still got it."

Bill thought of Matthew's brother and nodded seriously.

"And what about the freighters, Pa?"

"There's a freighter wagon train upcreek, see it?" Pa asked, pointing. "That'll be Alexander Major's company; they do most of the government hauling."

"What are they hauling?"

"Supplies for the forts and military posts out west, mostly," Pa said. "Uniforms, blankets, firearms. Flour and such. The goods they need come up the Missouri on steamers. Most all of it that's going on to Fort Riley and such places starts off at Fort Leavenworth. Quartermaster said they just outfitted an expedition from the War Department, bound out west to scout out a route for the railroad. All sorts of work here."

"I'd like to ride alongside those freighters one day," Bill said, a little dreamily. Pa laughed.

"Wouldn't surprise me if you did, son. Wouldn't surprise me a bit. Maybe I'll even go along with you. But right now we got to get ourselves down to that valley and find us our claim."

They rode down the sloping path and gradually found themselves in the midst of the wagons and camps. Bill would have liked to stop and question each party, discover the members' destination, and learn where they had started from. To hear the worst they feared might happen to them, and the best they hoped for. He envied them as the Alexander boys in Davenport had envied Bill himself. For though there was much to do, and great uncertainty about their future, Bill had already arrived home. This was Kansas Territory, and the Codys would be going no farther west. That alone made Bill all the more hungry to share in the experience of those for whom Fort Leavenworth was merely a gate to the frontier instead of a destination.

Pa showed no signs of slowing, however. He even urged them forward with greater speed as they neared the area where the Mormons were camped out. Bill knew enough to obey. Cholera had never stricken his family, but he had heard about its symptoms, from violent cramps and diarrhea to shriveled hands and feet and a deep, penetrating cold. At their worst, some even turned blue from the loss of fluids. Once sick, one could die in a matter of hours. He felt sorry for the Mormon families, but like Pa, he kept a safe distance.

Presently Pa stopped Little Gray and pulled out a roughly drawn map from his pocket. He studied it for several moments, occasionally looking around at the land to get his bearings.

"I believe the land Elijah was recommending to us is right up there," Pa finally said. He was pointing up the valley to a large hill on slightly wooded land in the distance. A river snaked its way around the hill. "What do you think, son?"

"Looks like a good place," Bill said, proud that Pa had asked his opinion. "Secluded, but close to water. Good view of the valley. Not too far from the fort. But we'll need to see it up close to really know."

Pa nodded approvingly. "You've got a good head on your shoulders, son."

Bill glowed inside. What a day it had been!

The horses walked slowly up the hill toward the spot Uncle Elijah had picked for them. In his mind Bill transformed the land, clearing it of trees and tilling the soil. His imagination erected a settler's shanty, then a larger, permanent homestead. His eyes picked out ruts not yet worn into the hill, a road his future was waiting to carve into the land. It fit. It all felt right.

"Well, son?" asked Pa.

"Now that I look, I can sure see it," Bill said. "It's home, Pa. No doubt about it. It's home."

As soon as the sun rose over their little campsite the next morning, Pa rode off on Little Gray to buy some supplies and to see if he could hire a man to help them build a shanty on their claim site. He left Bill alone with Orion at their camp. The land needed to be visibily occupied now, to help protect it from claim jumpers. Pa had heard stories of these pirates from Uncle Elijah, and he knew some of them would go to great lengths to steal away a prize piece of land if they thought they could get away with it. Bill knew Pa wasn't just trusting him not to wander off. He was trusting him to guard their new home. He was treating Bill like a man.

Though proud of his position as the defender of the claim, Bill secretly hoped no one would bother him. Turk had been left behind, to go with Ma and the girls to Uncle Elijah's farmhouse outside Weston. Pa had left him with a rifle, but still he was just one boy.

Forcing his thoughts away from claim jumpers, Bill built a fire. Then he fetched some water from a nearby spring and spent an hour or two clearing away the dead brush around the campsite. He spent time brushing Orion until his coat shone and his mane was free of tangles. It was good to keep occupied while waiting for Pa to return, though he enjoyed the feeling of being on his own.

Pa understood that about Bill. The need to be alone, to sit quietly out of doors, opening up one's mind to the vast possibilities of thought and imagination. What Ma and his sisters saw as idle daydreaming, Pa recognized as something more. All great accomplishments, Pa had once said, every invention that ever was, began with a thought. Everything that ever mattered—the Declaration of Independence, the expedition of Lewis and Clark, the great western expansion—it had all begun as a thought, as a recognition of potential. Joe Barnes's ma used to say that idle hands were the devil's playmate, but Bill and his pa knew better.

Everything that they would become, his family's future and well-being, already existed as a possibility in this uncultivated landscape. In ten years the columns of wagons lining the valley might be replaced with farms or churches. The cluster of trees and brush by the river could give way to a mill. This quiet hilltop would yield enough of itself to create a solid and joyful homestead for the Codys. Seated comfortably by the fire, Bill closed his eyes and imagined his future into reality.

The sound of several horses approaching snapped Bill out of his reverie. Claim jumpers! He scrambled to his feet and looked in the direction of the sound.

It was Pa, riding Little Gray and leading two wild-looking horses.

"Well, Bill, what do you think of my first Kansas purchase?" Pa asked with a grin as he climbed down from Little Gray's saddle. "Got us permission to graze horses here—I figured we'd better get some horses in the bargain!"

Bill could hardly find words and instead rushed

toward one of the horses, a light-colored sorrel. The horse startled at Bill's approach, then snorted and backed away. Bill inwardly chided himself. Knowing horses the way he did, he should never have rushed at the animal like that. In his excitement, he had momentarily forgotten this.

"Easy, Prince," Pa said in his soothing voice, getting off Little Gray. "They're not broken yet, Bill."

The first horse, Prince, calmed down. The second horse, a beautiful bay, watched Bill carefully, warning him with her lovely brown eyes not to approach.

He stood still as Pa untacked Little Gray and brushed him down. Bill looked from one new horse to the other, and both animals regarded him with cautious curiosity.

"Dolly will be the easier to break," Pa said, joining Bill by the horses. "That's clear. Prince has got a defiant streak in him—even the trader couldn't deny that. But he's a powerful creature, and beautiful to look at. If we ever manage to get a saddle on him, he might just be the fastest horse in Kansas Territory."

Bill nodded, never taking his eyes off Prince.

"So what do you think, Bill?" and Bill forced his gaze from the horse to look at his father.

"Think about what, Pa?" he asked.

"The horses, of course. Which one do you want?"

Bill felt his jaw drop as he stared at his father, terrified that Pa was simply making fun of him. Though

Bill had been riding Orion since he had learned to talk, the horse wasn't really his. No boy his age in LeClaire had his own horse. Even Sammy, in spite of his begging, had had to make due with Pa's horses.

Horses were serious business. They were expensive, and a family depended on them for any number of things. A good horse could be too easily spooked or ruined by a boy's mistakes. Bill had always taken great pains to learn as much as possible about handling horses, and deep down he knew he had a way with them. But he had never dared hope Pa would give him his own horse so soon. Especially not after what had happened to Sammy.

"Heavens, what a face, Bill!" Pa said, laughing. "Don't look so scared, son. I'm not joking with you. One of these horses is yours; all you got to do is say which one."

Bill didn't need even a second to decide.

"Prince. I'd like Prince, Pa."

Pa roared with laughter and clapped Bill on the back.

"I guessed as much," he said, grinning. "You rarely surprise me, boy, but you always delight me. What do you say we work these fellows for an hour or so before fixing supper?"

Of course, Pa had been right about Dolly. Though still nervous and skittish, she was soothed by Pa's gentle voice and hands and soon permitted a bridle to be placed over her nose. As Pa walked beside her and led her in large, slow circles around the camp, Bill worked on just getting close to Prince. The horse would let him approach, but as soon as he got so much as a glimpse of the rope in Bill's hand, he'd back away and snort angrily. Bill kept on trying, though, keeping his movements small and slow and mimicking the quiet, low voice his father used around horses.

Down the hill at a nearby camp, a young man watched as Bill struggled to get the frisky sorrel under control. After a while the man mounted his own horse and started up the hill toward the Codys' tent. Years later Bill would marvel at the ease with which this link to his family's past and herald of his own future rode so calmly into his world.

Chapter Nine

HORACE

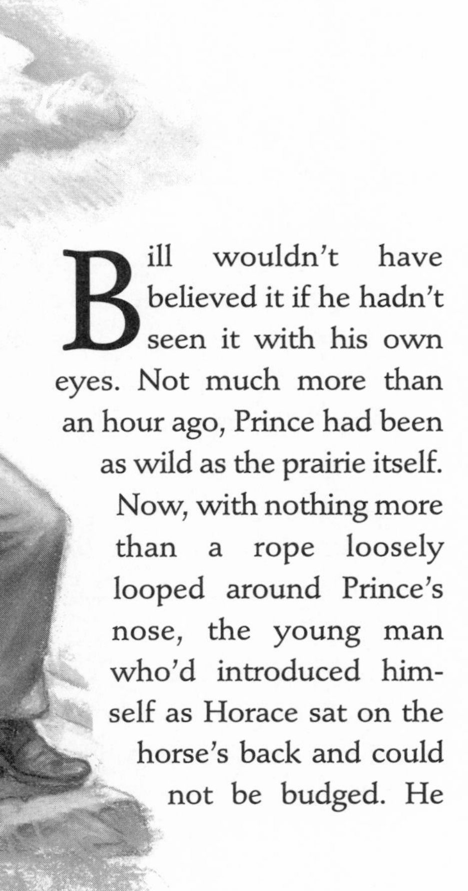

Bill wouldn't have believed it if he hadn't seen it with his own eyes. Not much more than an hour ago, Prince had been as wild as the prairie itself. Now, with nothing more than a rope loosely looped around Prince's nose, the young man who'd introduced himself as Horace sat on the horse's back and could not be budged. He managed the horse by that simple rope alone. Nothing Prince did could shake him—not bucking, not rearing, not careening wildly over the grass. Horace simply wrapped his legs around the horse's belly, held on to the rope, and sat tight.

Prince's strength was boundless, but Horace clearly had the edge in patience. He weathered each buck and kick as if it were no more than a hiccup, and eventually Prince quieted down and walked in circles around the camp. Horace leaned forward on Prince's back and murmured a few soft words, patting the horse on the neck. Then he dismounted and led the subdued horse to where Bill and his father were standing.

"He's all right," Horace said casually. "You'll be able to work him now."

"That was some trick," Pa exclaimed. "I'da thought it'd be a week at least before that horse would take so much as a blanket on his back. You're quite a horseman."

The man grinned.

"Been doing it most of my life," he said. "Do something that long, ain't no surprise you get pretty good at it."

Bill had sidled up to Prince and was stroking the horse gently. It seemed important, all of a sudden, that he show this man he wasn't completely inept with horses.

"Why don't you join us for some supper?" Pa said. "We were going to have some stew. Bought a whole potful from the wagonmaster of one of the major's freighters—it's more than Bill and I can eat. Seems like the least we can do for you."

"That'd be nice," said Horace.

"Glad to hear it," Pa said. "Did I introduce you to my son already? This here's Bill. And you can call me Isaac."

Horace reached out and shook Bill's hand as if Bill were a grown-up. Then he shook Isaac's hand. "Glad to meet ya."

He was the most magnificent-looking man Bill had ever seen. He was tall and powerfully built, with dark hair and eyes like Pa's. But he was clean shaven. He wore a wide-brimmed California sombrero and a buckskin jacket and britches decorated with blue and white beads and dangling fringe. Like most men of the frontier, he carried both a pistol and a hunting knife tucked into his belt. His face was leathery and tanned to a nut brown. His boots were high and worn.

Looking at Horace as he reclined by the fire and sharpened a stick with his knife, Bill thought, That is what I wish to be.

Bill would be the first to admit there was plenty he hadn't seen in the world, but he knew a genuine western man when he saw one. Reading books and newspapers about men like Kit Carson and Jim Bridger was one thing, but seeing a real frontiersman in the flesh was different. And Bill had never seen anyone with such an uncommon way with horses. The man seemed half horse himself. Even his name sounded like the animal. Did he dare hope Horace would stick around a few days and teach Bill a thing or two about horses?

"What's your business in these parts, Horace, if you don't mind my asking?" Pa said, ladling out a steaming bowl of the wagonmaster's stew and handing it to the young man.

"Don't mind at all," Horace said. "Been working out in California, catchin' wild horses and breakin' 'em. My outfit captured a fine herd over the summer, and we've been driving them east to sell."

"How many you got?" Pa asked.

"'Bout three hundred, give or take," was the answer, and Pa whistled.

"Guess that outfit is lucky to have you on board, judging from what I just saw," Pa said.

Horace shrugged modestly. "I just do what comes naturally," he said. "I was more or less raised on the back of a horse. Got so I just didn't care to do anything else. My pa was a good man, and a patient one, but he wanted me to take up some kind of trade instead of ridin' all day long. Finally forbade me from my horses altogether. We quarreled over that, and bein' a hotheaded youngster, I ran away."

Horace glanced at Bill, who was wide-eyed with wonder.

"Where did you go?" Bill asked. They were the first words he'd spoken since Horace had gotten off Prince.

"Went to sea for a spell," Horace said. "Then I settled in the Sandwich Islands, where I found work doing bareback riding tricks in a little circus."

It just kept getting better and better, Bill thought.

"After a few years I came east to California," Horace continued between spoonfuls of stew, "and I made a living training horses for the local mining companies. Then I met the boys," he said, gesturing in the direction of his camp with his head, "and started up mustanging with them. It's decent work and pays well when you sell the horses. It suits me, all in all."

"So you'll be heading back west when the horses are sold?" Bill asked, trying to mask his disappointment. He had hoped that Horace would stay around for a while.

"Eventually, but I ain't in no hurry," Horace said. Bill sighed with relief. "It's a loose outfit—we come and go as we please. I got relatives in Ohio I ain't seen for a long spell. Thought I might travel east and look 'em up. Had an uncle over in Weston, too, back when I was a kid. I expect I'll stop over and see if he's still livin' there."

"We've been staying in Weston, too," Pa said. "We could ask after your uncle when we go back, if you like. What is his name?"

"Elijah Cody," said Horace, and Bill nearly choked on his stew.

"Lord in heaven!" exclaimed Pa. "Elijah Cody?"

"Yes," said Horace, looking from father to son in puzzlement at their reaction. Pa spoke wonderingly.

"Why, if Elijah Cody is your uncle, then . . . you've got to be Sophia's boy, Horace Billings."

Horace looked as astonished as Bill felt. He nodded slowly.

"Well, Horace," said Pa, smiling broadly. "Meet your uncle Isaac Cody and your cousin Bill."

Horace threw back his head and laughed in delight. Bill simply stared, hardly able to believe his luck. This mustanger, this extraordinary western man who wore a real sombrero and buckskin jacket, whose horse sported a saddle studded with engraved silver medallions . . . this man was family!

"Don't you know my sister had given you up for dead?" Pa asked when they'd all calmed down. "We all thought you drowned, son, or worse."

"Well, here I am to prove you wrong," Horace boasted. Then, looking a little chagrined, he added, "I guess I figured word would get back to Ma one way or another. She okay?"

"Last I heard, both your folks were fine, Horace," Pa said. "Still living at the old place in Cleveland. Sophia will about lose her mind when she hears you're discovered, I reckon."

Horace nodded.

"How come you never wrote your folks to say you were okay?" Bill asked.

"Now that's none of our business, son," Pa said sternly, but Horace just shrugged.

"No matter," he said. "Didn't write 'cause I don't know how. And never really kept company with those who do."

Bill fell silent, thinking of his own experiences at school. Any time spent indoors had seemed like a waste, but it did help to know how to read and write. Imagine, he could do something Horace couldn't!

"Well, I been looking to hire a man to help me and Bill get up a little shanty on this piece of land," Pa said. "Don't suppose you'd be interested in the job?"

"Happy to do it for free," Horace replied. "Been a long time since I had family around."

Bill had to stop himself from exclaiming with pleasure.

"That's plenty kind of you, Horace," Pa said, smiling, "but I'll pay you all the same." Bill could see from Pa's face that he liked his nephew, and Bill was thrilled. Once somebody got off on the wrong foot with Pa, it could be some time before he changed his opinion of them. But once a person had earned Pa's respect, he had it forever. And Bill wanted Pa to respect Horace the way he already did himself.

"I better be getting back to my outfit tonight, before the boys run off with my gear, but I'll be back bright and early tomorrow. Three of us men'll have that shanty up in no time."

Bill flushed red at being included.

"Till tomorrow then," Pa said, and he and his nephew shook hands.

"Glad to meet you, Cousin Bill," Horace said, shaking Bill's hand next. "Maybe I can teach you a few tricks for Prince, if you've a mind."

"Oh yes!" said Bill, his face still flushed. It was just what he'd been hoping Horace would say.

Horace tipped his hat, then lightly sprang onto his horse and rode off toward his camp through the growing darkness.

Pa shook his head.

"Ain't that the darnedest thing," he said softly. "Imagine us running into Horace just like that, after all those years."

"How many years has he been gone, Pa?" Bill asked.

"About eight or nine, I suppose," Pa replied. "He was just about Sammy's age when he run off. Near broke his mama's heart. Seems like a decent man, but he should have got word back to her, just the same."

Bill had to agree with that. But otherwise, Horace seemed pretty near a perfect human being.

Bill fell asleep easily that night, his front warmed by the fire and his back cooled by the Kansas breeze. He dreamed he was Horace Billings, careening over the prairie on the bare back of a wild mustang, beholden to none.

Chapter Ten

GENTLIN'

★ ★ ★

Horace arrived early the next morning, just as he had promised. To Bill's delight, he'd brought his gear with him. He could see his outfit from the Codys' camp, he explained. If they ran off without him, at least he'd have his own things with him. Pa suggested Horace stay at their camp for a few days, and Horace readily agreed.

The shanty came along quickly with the three of them

working on it. It wasn't intended to be a permanent structure, so they didn't spend too much time worrying about making it windproof and watertight. They simply built a frame out of lumber Pa had bought that morning from some of the freighters and hammered boards around it. There was no fireplace, no shingles on the roof, which they'd covered with fresh-cut hay, and no windows. It was just a tiny cabin with a front door and single room. They didn't need to live in it, Pa explained. But the fact of the cabin, just standing there on the land, helped their claim of ownership.

Bill had never spent more than a half day with Pa before, away from Ma and the girls. In LeClaire Pa had occasionally taken Sammy along on a short stagecoach trip, and Bill had jealously accepted this as a privilege due the older son. But now Bill was the older son, and he could scarcely believe that he was here, in Kansas Territory, camping out with Pa on their claim, helping build their shanty with his own two hands. Part of Bill knew it was wrong to feel any pleasure in his new position as older, and only, son. It couldn't be right to find any good in Sammy's death. And if Sammy were still alive, it would be he, not Bill, who accompanied Pa to the claim, camped with him, and worked with him. It would have been Sammy who had met Horace. Sammy who had gotten Prince.

But I would give it all up in a second to have Sammy back, Bill thought. I would give it all to him and happily go back to the farmhouse to wait with Ma and the girls, in exchange for having Sammy alive. Except no one's offering that deal. Sammy isn't coming back, and I'm here.

In his heart Bill knew Sammy wouldn't want him feeling bad. Sammy would have wrung every last drop of enjoyment out of this time, and he would want Bill to do the same. It wasn't every day a boy got to go off with his pa and do something important and exciting. It wasn't every day a boy could eat hot stew by an open fire and neglect to wash his face before going to bed. It wasn't every day a boy could wear the same clothes, smelling of sweat and campfire smoke, with no complaint from anyone. He had to make the best of this time. He owed it to himself, and he owed it to Sammy. So Bill threw himself into every chore, every meal, and every moment with renewed vigor and excitement.

Horace also seemed to have an endless supply of energy. The shanty was mostly finished in two days, leaving plenty of time for Bill and Horace to work Prince together every day. Bill looked forward to these lessons as much as he looked forward to sleeping under the stars next to Pa each night.

"Now remember," Horace was saying, "these

animals are born bein' afraid of anything jumping onto their backs. Where these horses have been living, anything getting on their backs aims to kill 'em. And their withers here between the shoulder bones is real sensitive. That's why they buck so, but don't let that worry you. Only horse you got to worry about is one that don't buck the first time you get on him. That's a horse that ain't got spirit enough to bother with."

Bill listened, mesmerized, as Horace showed him how to hobble Prince, tying one foot up in a rope so the animal had to balance himself on three legs. Wild horses have a deep fear of being restrained or confined, the horseman explained, because they need to run to avoid and escape predators. The purpose of hobbling Prince was to teach him that he could be safe and remain unharmed even when his natural ability to run had been curtailed.

"Some cowboys don't bother with gentlin' a horse," Horace said, soothing the hobbled Prince with gentle strokes along the animal's withers. "They'll run a wild horse into a corral with a rope tied around the feet and let the horse run full speed till the rope is tight. Then *wham*—a somersault in the air, and that animal is down on his back. When he's down, you hog-tie him, saddle him, and climb on. When that horse has stopped buckin', you got yourself a green-broke animal. But you ain't got an animal that trusts you, and that's what I aim for when I break a horse. I want him to know who's master, sure, but just as important I want him to like me an' to feel safe with me. That's where gentlin' comes in."

After only four days of exposure to Horace and his workouts, Prince was already gentler than Bill had ever dreamed he would be.

They were working Prince in a relatively flat, grassy area below the campsite, warmed by the mellow late-afternoon sun.

"Your two most important tools to gentle him," Horace said, "are your hands and your voice. You treat your animal like you understand everything he's feeling. You watch out for him like you watch out for a little brother. When he's hot, you water him. When he's tired, you rub him down. When he's frustrated, you soothe him with your voice. And you sack him to take what's left of the spook out of him."

"Sack him?" asked Bill.

Horace nodded. "I use a real sack, but any old saddle blanket'll do. Best to start it when he's still hobbled. Take your sack in your hand like it's a washrag and rub him on his neck and shoulders, down his body. Walk all around him, rubbin' the sack on him and talkin' gentle. Once he's a bit used to it, you can dangle and flap it around his back and belly some. When you got a horse that's been well sacked while you're breakin' him, he won't ever be spooked by anything you're swinging around while you ride, or anything that's moving under him."

"Can I try?" asked Bill, and Horace handed him the sack he'd been using as he demonstrated.

Prince startled a bit as Bill approached him, but he quieted down as soon as the boy placed a reassuring hand on the horse's neck and said, "Whoa." Horace watched as Bill slowly and gently worked the sack around the horse's withers and belly. Prince was skittish at first, but eventually he stood quietly, occasionally turning his head and regarding Bill with his large, intelligent eyes.

"You got an uncommon touch, son," said Horace. "That horse is already thinking seriously about trusting you. There's fellas in my outfit I explained this to twenty times, and they still don't get it."

Bill glowed with pride and continued to rub the sack around his horse.

"That's pretty good work, there," Horace said eventually. "Pretty good. Prince looks 'bout ready for a break—what about you?"

Bill couldn't help but feel he should have noticed that by himself. If Prince was ever really going to be his horse, he had to know how to read him completely.

"Yes, sir," Bill said, and Horace laughed.

"You don't got to call me 'sir,'" he said, grinning.

"We're kin, after all. No one calls me 'sir' nohow; don't see why my own flesh and blood should."

Bill didn't know how else to show Horace the respect he felt for him. Good manners seemed the only way to convey his admiration to his cousin. But maybe good horsemanship would do just as well.

"Why don't you unhobble Prince and set him up with a bucket of water," said Horace. "And tell him he done good. Let him know you're proud of him. Folks who think horses don't understand simple praise don't know what they're talkin' about."

Bill did as Horace instructed, releasing Prince's hobbled front foot and stroking the horse's neck as he softly praised him. Prince made a soft nickering sound in response. When Bill had finished, he sat down next to Horace on the grass and took a drink from the canteen of water he was offered.

"You're gonna have a fine horse there, Bill," said Horace. "From the look of it now and how you handle him, you're gonna have a fine animal indeed."

"I sure hope so," Bill said. "I ain't never had a horse of my own before."

"'Twas generous of your pa, that's for certain," Horace said, taking a long drink from the canteen and supplementing it with a sip from another container he produced from his pocket. "He must have a lot of faith in you, boy, to give you such a fine animal."

"I guess," Bill said. "'Cept there is one thing that confuses me."

"What's that?" Horace asked.

Bill paused a moment, then told Horace the story of how Sammy had died.

"So considering all that, I got to kind of wondering why he'd give me a horse of my own, one that ain't even broke yet."

"It's pretty clear to me," Horace said. "To run this claim, he needs to break some horses. Seems the best way to avoid having a twelve-year-old boy who can't handle a wild horse is to raise an eight-year-old boy who learned himself how to."

In a muddled way, what Horace said made sense to Bill. Pa's not going to let it happen again, he thought. Looking downhill at the valley still crowded with prairie schooners, their shadows lengthened by the late-day sun, Bill thought how much more they would be depending on horses here. In LeClaire many of their needs could be provided for right in town, just a few streets away from their house. But there was no town here in Salt Creek, not yet. And there might not be one for some time to come. By giving him Prince, Pa was telling Bill that he was going to rely on him in their new home. He would be taking on new responsibilities, like any family man.

"And you got the gift, son," Horace continued.

"Believe you me, I don't say that to just anybody. But you listen, you got patience, and you got the gentle touch. And you like horses, I can tell."

"I sure do," Bill said eagerly. "If I could figure out a way to spend my whole life around 'em, I surely would."

"Plenty of ways to do that," Horace said. "Mustanging or being a vaquero. Trappin' and tradin'. Even those dragoons back at the fort get to spend half their lives around horses. Though those uniforms don't look none too comfortable."

"But I'm not even nine yet," Bill said a little sheepishly.

"What's eight, nine? Just numbers," said Horace, taking another sip from his flask before slipping it under his shirt. "A true man does what's required of him when it's time. Eight or eighty, don't matter. I can see in your eyes, Bill, that you're the kind of man who'll always do what's needed when folks need something doin'. Right now, you got a homestead to build and land to clear. Next year, who knows? You could be riding scout-side with one of Russell's wagon trains."

"Doesn't seem possible," Bill said. All the same, he imagined himself riding at the head of a thirty-wagon train, heading out west on the Santa Fe Trail to bring supplies to Colonel Kearney's dragoons.

"When opportunity comes knockin', you'll know

it," Horace reassured him, handing him the canteen again. "I know horses most, but I know men, too, and I'm tellin' you, son, you got no cause for worrying. You're gonna do exciting things, and people gonna know who you are."

The words of encouragement from his new hero were almost more than Bill could bear, and he gave relief to his feelings by draining the canteen dry.

Though four days of Horace's company had not been nearly enough for Bill, the time had come for father and son to return to Weston to consult with Uncle Elijah. News traveled slowly in Kansas Territory, and Pa had no way of knowing how close the bill was to being signed. He wanted to know the moment it happened, as he wanted to be among the first to officially file a claim. Now that they had found their new home, Pa had no intention of losing the land by being unprepared.

To Bill's delight, Pa had asked Horace to stay on their land for the several days they'd be away, and Horace had agreed. It was one thing to invite Horace to camp out with them a few days, but quite another to entrust the protection of the claim to him. Of course, the fact that Horace was family made all the difference.

Horace would watch over the claim for as long as it took Bill and Pa to take the ferry to Weston, find Uncle Elijah, get the latest news on the bill, and bring Elijah over to Kansas Territory to see the claim and meet his long-lost nephew. Horace said the whole thing would save him a trip across river and that he'd just as soon relax around camp anyway, but Bill still thought it was awfully generous of him to stand guard over their claim while they were gone.

Pa had agreed to let Bill accompany Horace to Rively's trading post, where Horace needed to buy some food supplies before Bill and Pa left for Weston. Rively's was about a mile east of the claim site, almost halfway to Fort Leavenworth. The store sold a little bit of everything and also served as a hub for the latest news and rumors making their way into the territory.

A simply built log structure, the store had a large porch with many barrels and boxes that served as furniture for customers who wished to sit and socialize. Most customers did. Bill had heard a little about the place from Pa, so he knew it wouldn't much resemble the general store in LeClaire, but nothing prepared him for the mobs of men milling all around, shouting, singing, and drinking whiskey.

Judging by the crowds gathered there, it seemed this was the most popular place in all of Kansas Territory. Horace went inside to make his purchases, and Bill stayed outside, a little distance from most of the crowd, watching over Orion and Horace's mount, Rogue.

By the store's front entrance, two men were arguing. They were dressed like farmers, and though they were yelling at each other, Bill had trouble making out what they were saying. Their voices rose louder and louder, and before long they had come to blows. No one bothered to intervene, but a small crowd gathered around the fighting men and cheered. Someone began taking bets, waving a handful of cash in the air. A fist connected with one man's mouth, and Bill thought he saw several teeth fly into the air.

Though he felt he shouldn't be watching, Bill couldn't help staring at the tussling men, who were cheered on by the crowd whenever either threw a punch. Men fought in LeClaire, too, but Bill had never seen such a spectacle made of a brawl. The shouting audience seemed almost cheerful, as if the fight were entertainment being presented for their amusement.

Things are just plain different here in Kansas Territory, Bill said to himself. I better make sure never to forget it.

"Ruffians," said Horace. "Pay 'em no mind."

Bill couldn't stop himself from jumping slightly. He'd been so absorbed in watching what was going on that he hadn't seen Horace come out of the store.

His cousin barely seemed to notice the fight at all as he loaded some small bags of sugar and flour into Rogue's saddlebags.

"What do you think they're fighting about?" Bill asked, unable to tear his eyes away.

"Could be anything at all," Horace said. "A claim, a business deal gone bad. Whose horse is faster. Some men just can't communicate no other way. They'll fight you just for sayin' good morning. You heard anybody say law and morality never crossed the Mississippi? It's men like that they're talking about. They'll duke it out till one of 'em falls down, and it'll all pass on by."

"Coupla cowboys," a gravelly, slurring voice called. "Coupla cowboys, ain'tcha?"

Bill realized with a sick feeling that the voice was directed at them.

"What of it?" Horace said coolly, turning to face the man who had spoken.

"Where you from, stranger?" the man said, none too pleasantly. He could have been almost any age, with his deeply lined face and bad teeth. His hair was thinning and his pants and untucked shirt were worn almost through. It looked like neither the man nor his clothes had seen soap in a good long while. Bill noticed the man's heavy movements and thickened speech, which he guessed meant too much to drink.

"California," Horace said. "But maybe you ain't never heard of it."

The man sneered. "Come here to get yourself a prime piece of our land, didya?" he said accusingly.

"I'm no homesteader. Ain't got no interest in your land or anything on it," Horace said. "Specially you."

This stopped the man for a moment.

"That one's kind of short to be a cowboy," the man said finally, sneering in Bill's direction.

"Not from where I'm standin'," Horace said.

Bill felt frozen in place, unsure what to do.

"You callin' me a liar?" the man growled.

"Hard to say, drunk as you are," Horace replied pleasantly. "Could be you're just plain stupid."

"Now you jes' askin' for it," the man said, scowling.

"Just tryin' to hurry things along," Horace explained. "You been tryin' to pick a fight with me since you caught sight of me. I'm happy to oblige, but let's get on with it. I ain't got all day."

Horace stood at the ready, looking powerful and capable. The surly man didn't take even a second to make up his mind.

"Durn cowboys," he muttered, picking his way back through the crowd.

"Drunken squatters," said Horace, shaking his head. "Nothin' like free land and cheap whiskey to bring out the worst in a man."

"Why did he want to fight you?" Bill asked. Horace shrugged.

"Too mean to know better or too drunk to care," he replied. "Like I said, some men just don't know any other way." Horace got into the saddle, and Bill got on Orion. They left the trading post behind, the two men still fighting.

After a time, Horace said, "Always stand your ground, Bill. You'll find you're made of better stuff than most, if you just stand your ground."

It sounded so easy when Horace said it. But looking behind to the crowded store, the atmosphere ricocheting between cheerfulness and violence, Bill wondered how he'd ever learn to hold his own on this side of the Missouri.

As the sun began to set over the Missouri River, the scene from Rively's earlier that day receded in Bill's mind. He and Pa had left Horace safely installed on their claim with the understanding that they'd return in two days' time. They'd arrived at the Fort Leavenworth wharf just in time to catch the next ferry to Weston. Like most steamers making the river crossing from west to east, the ferry was not crowded at all, so Bill was able to enjoy the feel of the breeze, which smelled fresh and slightly muddy, in peace. He spent most of the trip in quiet contemplation, his face to the river, his back warmed by the sun, watching the land slip by.

"Pa?" Bill asked, as the ferry rounded the bend and Weston loomed into view.

"Yes, son?" said Pa, looking unusually happy.

"Horace says a man should always stand his ground."

"That's right," Pa replied.

"But Uncle Elijah says sometimes you gotta keep your head low and stay outa trouble."

Pa looked a little surprised, and Bill wondered if he'd just given away his eavesdropping on Pa and Uncle Elijah. But Pa either didn't notice or chose not to mention it.

"Well, yes," he said after a moment. "Elijah does say that."

"Which one is right?" Bill asked. "'Cause it don't seem like a person can do both at the same time."

"What are you asking for, Bill?" asked Pa. "You got something on your mind?"

"Not really," Bill said. "It's just . . . well, I hear folks talkin' about the way things'll be after this bill is passed an' all, and it's just hard to know who to believe, that's all."

"Are you asking me if there's going to be trouble about the slavery vote, Bill? And what I'm going to do about it?"

Bill nodded, hardly able to keep his father's eye. There was a long pause.

"Well, we're the men of the family, son, and

now that you mention it, it does seem right we talk it over."

Bill felt swept over with relief. He looked his father full in the face and waited.

"I been listening to what folks are saying, and it does seem like things might get a bit rough where this vote is concerned," Pa said. "And maybe I was a little blind to that before. But that's all right, and no harm done. Once that bill has passed, son, I don't imagine it'll be more than a month or two before they take that vote, and once that's over, so are the troubles." He looked at the Weston landing, looming closer. "I think what Horace and your uncle Elijah say both make sense. Sometimes a man's got to stand his ground, and sometimes he's got to duck his head and bite his tongue. Ain't no man can know which to do until he's faced with the situation. And when that time comes, if it does, you and I'll just have to use the good judgment God gave us. What do you think about that, son?"

Bill nodded.

"I think that's just fine, Pa," he said. "When the time comes, we'll know what we must do."

"Good boy," Pa said, giving Bill a clap on the back. "You're my good boy, Bill."

The steamboat's whistle shrieked loudly as the boat slowed to a stop. They had arrived. The steamboatmen busied themselves in securing the ferry. Bill and Pa collected Little Gray and Orion from the lower level and led the horses down the gangplank. It hadn't been easy for Bill to leave Prince behind, but he knew Prince was still far too green to make the ferry trip without spooking, and anyway, the horses were supposed to be left grazing on the claim. And he had left him in Horace's capable hands, after all.

Bill tightened Orion's girth and hoisted himself easily into the saddle. But before he and Pa could begin the short ride up Main Street to Uncle Elijah's townhouse, Bill was surprised to catch sight of Uncle Elijah himself making his way toward them.

"Isaac!" Uncle Elijah called. Pa had seen his brother, too, and waved to him.

"I was just about to get on the ferry and come looking for you," Uncle Elijah said, slightly out of breath. "'Twas a bit of good fortune I spotted you."

"Nothing's wrong, I hope," Pa said, and Uncle Elijah shook his head.

"Quite the opposite," he replied. "I've just gotten word that President Pierce has signed the bill, Isaac. Kansas is officially open now, and word is spreading fast. I wanted to get the news to you so you could file the paperwork on the claim."

"He's signed it!" Pa repeated. "So it's done, just like that! I expect I better get myself back across the river quick, and beat the crowd to the claims office."

"Did you find the land I recommended?" Uncle Elijah asked, and Pa nodded.

"We sure did, and it was everything you said, Elijah. Actually, everything went just as you said it would. Got me the grazing permission and hay contract, and already built a little cabin on the land."

"You didn't leave it alone, did you?" Uncle Elijah asked sharply.

Pa chuckled. "Nope. I found someone real trustworthy to watch it for us, and you ain't gonna be half surprised when I tell you who it is!"

"The most important thing is to get back to Kansas as quick as possible," Uncle Elijah said, ignoring Pa's excitement. "This ferry is continuing on upriver. If we ride fast, we can probably get the horses down to Rialto in time for the last ferry over tonight. I'll come along with you, to make sure the paperwork will go through quickly, if you think Bill here can get himself to the farmhouse to let your family know what's happening. Can he follow the directions if I draw out a map?"

"Of course I can," said Bill, bristling slightly. He'd gotten used to Pa and Horace treating him like a grown-up this past week. Uncle Elijah obviously still considered him a boy.

Uncle Elijah quickly sketched a little map, which he handed to Bill.

"Just follow this road here out of Weston. It's a

straight two-mile ride, and we're the first farm you'll come to. Yellow house."

"I understand," Bill said. "I can find it easy."

"Thank you, son," Pa said, climbing onto Little Gray. "You let your ma know the bill has been signed, and that we've gone back over to file the claim. We'll get it done as quick as we can, but in the meantime see that the wagons get packed up and made ready to go."

"Okay, Pa," Bill said. Pa and Uncle Elijah were already turning their horses around, and with a quick wave, Pa took Little Gray to a trot, and the brothers were off toward Rialto.

Bill gave Orion a quick squeeze with his legs, and the horse pricked up his ears and began to walk. Before turning up Main Street, Bill looked across the river at Kansas. It was officially open to settlers now, just like that. Not for the first time, Bill felt surprised at how some of life's most important moments just slipped in quietly when you least expected them.

He mulled this thought over for a moment, then started uphill in the direction of Elijah's farmhouse. His family was waiting, and he had news.

Chapter Eleven
CROSSING OVER

★ ★ ★

It seemed like they were all talking at once. Even Ma, usually so restrained, talked over Martha when she asked Bill to describe the claim. Bill provided all the details he could muster about the claim, the surrounding landscape, and the fort. He did not tell them about Rively's, except to say there was a store about a mile away.

Though Uncle Elijah's farmhouse had a separate

parlor, the Codys had congregated in the kitchen to listen to Bill's news. Aunt Louisa and Lucinda, Uncle Elijah's daughter, had not yet returned from a shopping expedition to Weston, and had taken along their serving lady, so Ma busied herself at the stove preparing dinner as she listened to what Bill had to tell the family.

Bill cast a few glances at Julia as he talked. He'd expected her to be more excited, both at the prospect of the claim and at his own return. Turk had hurled himself against Bill in ecstasy at his return and had refused to leave his side since. Julia, on the other hand, barely seemed to notice he'd been gone. Now she sat across from him at the table with her head bent over a bit of mending, and she seemed to be only half listening. He couldn't help feeling a little hurt at her subdued reaction. But then, as he began to describe the arrival of Horace, he shot her another look. She was still hunched over her sewing, but Bill noticed all at once that her hands were quite still. She wasn't sewing anything. Bill realized then that Julia was being very guarded, permitting herself the most reserved, most ladylike, reaction to his news. When he thought that for each day he'd spent outside with Pa, Horace, and Prince, Julia had been stuck in this house with girl chores, he felt a sudden flare of love for her. He also felt a little guilty at his new freedom that Julia, three years his senior, was not being granted. He resolved to make his life at the claim sound a little less thrilling when describing it to his sister.

"What does that mean, Bill?" Eliza Alice was saying, as she held sleeping Mary Hannah carefully on her lap. "If Pa is his uncle, does that mean Horace is our brother?"

"Our cousin, Eliza Alice," Martha corrected, while helping Ma get supper ready. "His mother is Pa's sister, Sophia."

"Is he a bad man?" asked Nellie eagerly, and Ma and Martha made noises of disapproval.

"Nellie, why on earth would you ask such a thing?" said Martha.

Nellie pouted. "You said there could be bad men there, Martha," she began.

Martha made a dismissive noise. "Not in our family, Nellie. A Cody is a Cody, after all."

"Billings," Bill corrected.

"Billings by birth," Martha said matter-of-factly, "but still a Cody by blood."

"And how did this Horace come to find himself in your camp, Bill?" Ma asked.

"He rode up one afternoon, just like that. Pa had bought some new horses that weren't yet broke, and one of 'em was pretty wild, and Horace hopped right on his back, nice as you please, and no matter what that horse did, he stuck on like nothing doing."

"Pa bought new horses?" Julia asked, finally looking up.

Bill smiled, pleased she had asked. "Two of 'em," he said. "A sorrel and a bay. And the sorrel is a wild one! But Horace gentled him, just like that. His name is Prince, and Pa says he's mine!"

He regretted the words as soon as they were out of his mouth. Ma had frozen in place by the stove. She spoke without turning around to look at him.

"Pa gave you a horse of your own?"

"Yes, Ma," Bill said. Julia gave him an anxious look, which Bill returned.

"And it's a wild, unbroken animal?" Ma continued, her voice dangerously quiet.

"Well, he's not wild anymore, Ma, not leastwise. Horace has been working miracles with him."

"Your pa gave you a horse to break," Ma repeated. Julia glanced back and forth from her mother to her brother.

"Yes, Ma," Bill said. After a moment, he added, "I reckon he thought about it good and long."

Ma didn't respond to this. The family sat in silence for several moments. Bill felt thankful when Nellie piped up with another question.

"What's the other horse's name, Bill?" she asked eagerly.

"Dolly," Bill said, tearing his eyes from his mother's rigid back. "She's a sweet little bay, Nellie.

I think she'll be real gentle. You'll like petting her."

"I want to ride her!" Nellie cried, and Julia shushed her.

"You're too small for that, Nellie, and you know it," Julia said. "Let's have no more talk of it."

"What's it been like staying here?" Bill asked quickly, eager to change the subject.

"Aunt Louisa runs a lovely, proper household," Martha said, beginning to set the table. "And Cousin Lucinda has been most gracious sharing her home with us."

Julia made a little face when Martha turned away, and Bill laughed inwardly at this glimpse of the old Julia. Obviously, there wasn't much love lost between Julia and Uncle Elijah's family.

"But what are they like?" Bill pressed. He'd left for Kansas Territory directly from the Weston townhouse and hadn't even met his aunt or cousin.

"Aunt Louisa is quite elegant, with beautiful manners," Martha said after a moment. "And Lucinda . . . has lovely clothes."

"Are they nice?" Bill asked.

"They are extremely accommodating," Martha said.

Bill began to get the idea. It seemed that Martha, too, was looking forward to leaving them behind, even if she hadn't come right out and said it.

Bill had wondered about his aunt and his cousin

Lucinda, who was probably somewhere between Julia and Martha in age. He had guessed they might be as serious and stiff as his Uncle Elijah. Not that he wasn't grateful to his uncle. There was little doubt that Uncle Elijah had been extremely helpful so far in the Kansas Territory—his advice, time and time again, had proved right on the money. Strange to think that he was actually Pa's younger brother.

What would his and Sammy's relationship have been like, had they both grown into adults? Would Sammy ever have accepted advice from his younger brother unconditionally, as Pa did from Uncle Elijah? Would their friendship have grown into something like the subdued but respectful kinship Pa and Uncle Elijah shared? Bill liked to think that they would have listened to each other—that Sammy would have listened to him—but in an altogether warmer way.

Bill's attention turned to the plate of hot roast chicken Ma placed before him. He glanced up at her, but her face was unreadable. He tried to think of something to say as she sat down.

"We should be sure that we're set to go first thing in the morning, Ma," he said at last.

Ma took a moment before replying.

"There won't be much to pack," she said. "Just the bags we unloaded for our stay in Weston."

"I can ready the teams," Bill said carefully. Ma didn't remark this time on the prospect of Bill working with the horses and oxen. It wasn't as if there was a choice. Bill was the only logical person to do it. In anticipation of their getting under way, George Yancey had already gone down to the river to stand in line for a ferry. Even with the connection to Uncle Elijah, it might be a day or more before a place could be secured for both the family and their wagons and teams. In the meantime, the man's work would fall to Bill.

Somehow or other, Bill thought, Ma was going to have to realize that things had to be different in Kansas. Whatever might have been expected of, or forbidden to, Bill back in Iowa simply wasn't going to apply in the new territory. Things had changed. They weren't in Iowa anymore. Bill wasn't just a younger brother now. They were a family of settlers, and Bill was the older son. This meant he'd be taking on big responsibilities. He knew this, and Pa knew it, and even Horace knew it.

But how Ma would come to know it, and accept it, was another matter altogether.

George had sent a message just after breakfast the next day that the family would get a place on a ferry that afternoon. They were ready to go. Bill would be driving one of the prairie schooners himself, and Ma the carriage. Bill arranged for the messenger, a young man from Weston, to drive the second prairie schooner to the ferry for a small fee, and he felt proud to have made this arrangement himself. Again, Ma said nothing when Bill got into place on the little driver's bench of the prairie schooner. Like most boys, Bill had been taught to drive an ox team from an early age, and though he hadn't much experience doing so without Pa at his side, he felt confident that he could guide the heavy wagon through Weston without much difficulty.

If the Weston landing had seemed crowded when they had first arrived in town, it was now a mob scene. Word of the bill's passage was spreading rapidly, and as Uncle Elijah had predicted, folks from all corners of the States were rushing to the new territory to stake a claim. Families gathered anxiously at their prairie schooners, and bands of men roved back and forth. From every direction came the bellowing of livestock and the shouts of children. If he hadn't been so eager to return to Prince and Horace, Bill might have enjoyed it.

Ma was most certainly not enjoying herself. She stood between the two prairie schooners, with Martha and the girls in a tight circle around her. Even Julia looked uncomfortable amidst the frenzied movements and sounds erupting all around. Turk, who was tied securely to one of the wagon wheels, strained and whined, frustrated that he could not investigate any of the smells drifting by.

"Should be just another hour or so," George said reassuringly to Ma. He had been looking out for them at the landing. "Maybe even less. But it can't hurt to keep remindin' 'em we're here. You be okay if I go and check again?"

"Yes, thank you, George," Ma said. George nodded, and pushed his way back through the crowd.

Bill busied himself checking on the horses and oxen, stopping long enough with each one to give a reassuring pat and some soothing words. He knew it was important to keep all of them calm in the midst of the frenzied activity around them.

As he rechecked the yokes, Bill became aware of two men who were walking a bit unsteadily, and talking loudly to each other. They paused ten or fifteen feet from the Codys' wagons. Occasionally Bill was able to pick out some words. Kansas. Blackhearts. Abolitionists.

Sometimes they seemed to be harassing particular people. Other times they just seemed intent on making as much noise as possible. This was made more worrisome by the fact that both men carried pistols. They drew closer, and it seemed they might actually pass right by the Codys' wagons without saying anything, but one stopped when Turk lunged against his rope lead and barked furiously.

One man drew his gun and pointed it at the dog. Bill wanted to jump forward and put himself between Turk and the gun, but he forced himself to remain still.

"Turk, quiet," he said loudly. Turk stopped barking but was growling and straining forward.

"Try it, you mangy cur," the man said to Turk. "An' you'll git a bullet between your eyes."

"Lie down, Turk. Quiet." Bill was forceful but calm.

Turk lay down but continued to bare his teeth in ferocious warning.

Bill caught sight of Julia's face. She looked pale and clutched Mary Hannah tightly. Ma stood rigid, her face a tight mask.

"Tha's right," said the second man. "You a smart boy. But you talk funny."

Both men laughed.

"Yep, sounds like a fancy eastways accent," said the man who had threatened Turk, putting his gun away. "I knew it—this a damn Yankee dog. Ought to shoot it down right now. You all ain't welcome here, you know that, don'tcha?" Bill said nothing. He didn't know which was worse, speaking up or remaining silent.

"Tha's right," said the other man, fumbling around for his own pistol. "Kansas is Missouri territory. We don't need no foreigners with their upstart politickin'. We lived in Weston all our lives, and we don't aim to hand over no land now. Yankees is bein' turned back at the borders, and the ones who get through get themselves some serious problems. A bunch of womenfolk and a little boy ain't got no chance. Why don't you save us all a whole mess a trouble and go on back east right now?"

There was a brief silence. The first man looked suddenly irritated and drew his gun again.

"You heard what the man said," he stated in an ugly tone. "Whatcha waitin for? Get on outa here."

The conversation with Pa on the ferry came suddenly to Bill's mind. There was a time to speak up and a time to back off, and you wouldn't know which was right until the time came. Bill hadn't realized the time would come so soon, but here it was. Pa had treated him like a man, and now he was going to have to act like one. He thought quickly. He couldn't let Turk loose. The men probably would shoot the dog, just as they'd said. Both of them seemed like they might do violence without much in the way of second thoughts. But there was something weak about them, too, something that reminded him of the man Horace had cowed, something about their faces that struck Bill. Something that told him these men could be outtalked, too.

The words came to him without effort, as if they'd just been waiting for him to notice them hanging in the air.

"You say you're Weston men," Bill said as loudly and evenly as he could. "Then I'm sure you know my uncle Elijah Cody. We're heading across river to meet him this very day. I'm sure he'd be plenty disappointed if we didn't show up, and he'd sure want to know the reason why."

The two men looked at each other. Like most people who lived in Weston, they knew Elijah's name and reputation.

"How do we know you ain't makin' it up?" asked the first man. "Any fool could say he's kin to Cody, or to Atchison himself. Like as not it's a stinkin' lie."

"Could be," said Bill, trying to imitate the almost pleasant tone Horace had used with the troublemaker back at Rively's. "Only one way to find out at the moment. Try to run us off, you'll find out for sure."

The two men stood staring at Bill. Ma and the girls still stood, completely frozen, between the two wagons.

"I need sumthin' to drink," said the first man. Without another word he walked off. The other followed close behind him.

As he realized the danger had passed, Bill had an overwhelming urge to throw up. He caught sight of

Ma's face, drawn and white. He walked over to her, his legs feeling like jelly.

"Those men had guns, Bill," she said.

"I know, Ma," he replied carefully.

"They might have done something."

"I know, Ma," Bill repeated. "But they didn't."

"No," Ma said. "They didn't." She looked surprised when she said it, and Bill knew all of a sudden that he wasn't in trouble with her. Not really. Because he'd done the right thing. He'd done what Pa would have done, and even through her fear, Ma could see that.

George suddenly appeared, unaware that anything had gone on.

"They're ready for us," he said. "We gotta go right now. Bill, why don't you take the first team and I'll lead the second. Best get the children up now, Mrs. Cody. It's gonna be crowded."

The family was suddenly more ready than ever to move on. Bill looked across the muddy water, and Kansas beckoned like a vision. He hoped their troubles would be left here on this side of the Missouri River. And if they weren't, he hoped he'd be up to handling them.

Chapter Twelve

A New Home

Bill could see that Ma was disappointed in the little shanty cabin where they would make do while the permanent house was being built. But she made no complaint. Pa's claim had gone through without a hitch. The traveling was over now, and they had come home. Ma busied herself unloading a small box of dishes and some bedding and putting a cloth over the crude table Horace had built while they were away.

Still, the shanty was small and dark, particularly when all of them were inside. It was just as well, Bill thought, that it was early summer and, when the weather permitted, they could do their cooking and eating out of doors, and spend as little time as possible inside the shanty. Besides, they had to build a house, and that meant the shanty would stand empty for a good part of each day.

Kansas was proving a generous land. Unlike the true prairie regions on the western edges of the territory, Salt Creek had plenty of trees to provide lumber for fences and buildings. And as they cut the trees, they would be clearing land for crops.

With that generous land came generous neighbors. The very first morning after the Codys settled into their shanty, a doctor named Hathaway rode up. He had filed for a nearby claim. Bill liked Dr. Hathaway at once, with his tanned and weathered face and his honest, open way of talking.

"Yessiree, this is fine land," Dr. Hathaway said after he introduced himself. "'Tweren't no exaggerating goin' on. And you got yourself a pretty claim here, Cody. I tell ya, if I'd seen it first, I woulda taken it myself."

Pa smiled, looking pleased. Bill felt proud, too, because he'd been there first with Pa, when they'd staked their claim, and had seen it was a good place.

"We're settled in good time, as long as the weather holds," Pa said. "Only halfway through June now. If nothing goes wrong, we ought to have our house up and the land cleared before fall."

"Well, I'll tell you what," said Dr. Hathaway. "Seems we could be of help to each other here. You give me a hand with my house, and I'll give you a hand with yours. And since you got so many more kin needin' to keep warm and dry, I say we start with your house."

"I sure do appreciate it," Pa said. Uncle Elijah had returned to his business dealings in Weston after Pa had gotten the claim filed, and he knew he could sorely use the extra help, even with Horace and George there. "And I'll be glad to return the favor. Hear that, Mary? We'll be out of that shanty in no time."

Ma beamed like the spring prairie sun. Bill could barely remember the last time he'd seen his ma smile that broadly.

With so many people pitching in, it was a real house raising, the kind Bill had read about. While Bill and Horace cleared the house site of brush and grass, Pa and Doc Hathaway marked the tallest and straightest trees they could find and set to cutting them down. George had converted one of the prairie schooners into a durable farm wagon, and they used it to haul the lumber back to the site.

When all the timber was finally cut, sorted, and neatly stacked, the house was ready to be raised.

Ma and Martha had baked plenty of corn bread and put up pots of steaming coffee along with jugs of cold water, while the men set to wedging the log walls of the house into place. It was hard work, and dangerous, too, because logs could slip and crush a person if they weren't handled carefully.

Pa laid the first row of logs on the ground in a square. Near the end of each log he carved a notch with his hatchet. As he and George lowered the second row of logs right on top of the first row, each log fit neatly onto the notch. They continued laying row after row of logs, right up to where the roof would begin. Now they had a log box that was open on the top, but with no way to get in until Pa cut a door and windows through the walls. Then Bill started the chinking, taking lumps of mud and using them to plaster the spaces between the logs so the wind and the rain wouldn't get in. Horace and George cut long planks of wood for the roof, while Doc made shakes of bark to nail into place for a good set of roof shingles.

Meanwhile Pa was already at work with his adz splitting off thin slabs of wood from the remaining saw logs to create smooth, flat boards for the floor. When all the wood had been cut, Pa would lay these boards one next to the other and secure them into place, and Ma would have herself a new puncheon floor.

It all came together with startling quickness. In four days, a house stood where there had been only grass and brush before. The one-story house of logs looked so neat and tightly built, Bill could hardly believe they'd made it themselves. Except for the missing door, which Pa would make tomorrow, Bill thought the structure looked as sturdy as Fort Leavenworth itself. Julia seemed especially impressed, Bill couldn't help noticing.

Even Horace was amazed.

"Folks I keep with live in the outdoors, mostly, or move from tent to cabin," Horace explained to Bill. "That Hathaway is a good man. And ain't it great to have a doctor as a neighbor! You Codys are gonna do just fine here."

Bill was glad to hear Horace say so. Here was a man who had been places, who had seen parts of the world most boys had never even heard of. Done things most only dreamed about, Bill included. When Horace said that something was so, Bill took his word as fact.

"Will you be staying with us a spell, Horace, now that the house is done?" Bill asked. Horace shook his head, and Bill tried not to show his disappointment.

"I already stayed a lot longer than I planned," he

said. "If I'm gonna make it to Cleveland and back before winter to see my people, I'd best get started now. George says he's planning on taking the ferry back tomorrow. I reckon I'll go along with him."

"We sure do appreciate everything you've done for us," Pa said earnestly, joining them.

"It's nothin'," Horace said. "Enjoyed myself. Specially spendin' time with this young horseman here. Bill's got a real way with horses, I tell ya. I'm lookin' forward to seein' what he makes of that young sorrel horse you give him."

Ma's face froze. Bill knew she and Pa had had words about Prince the first morning they were all on the claim. The subject had not been raised since, but it still hung heavy in the air. Each time Bill climbed into the saddle, Ma would hurry into the shanty, as if unable to bear the sight of it. Ma didn't speak of it to Bill, but she didn't need to. The fear she felt for him was as plain as day.

George and Horace got under way not long after the sun rose. George carried a packet of letters for the Codys' friends back in Iowa, and Horace carried another letter for his mother in Cleveland. As he watched his cousin swing easily into the saddle, Bill felt a pang of oncoming loneliness so sharp, he almost cried out.

The whole family stood outside to say good-bye, and almost everyone seemed to feel the loss of their cousin, and of George, who had been a good companion to them. George was on his horse and ready to go. Pa reached up and shook the hired man's hand.

"I thank you, George. Couldn't have done it without you."

"Good luck to you, Mr. Cody," George replied. "And I'll make sure these letters get back to Iowa safe."

"And I'll deliver your message to Elijah and your letter to my ma," Horace said from atop Rogue.

"I do appreciate it," Pa said. "And we sure would like to know how you're getting on, and where you are."

"Don't you worry," Horace said with a laugh. "You'll hear about me, probably more than you've a mind to."

"Do you promise?" Bill asked, his voice sounding funny over the lump in his throat.

"I do indeed," Horace said. "Who knows? I may even get the chance to stop over on my way back west."

Bill could feel a grin spreading across his face.

"There will always be a room and a hot meal for you here," Pa said, and Horace smiled.

"I do thank you, Uncle."

He began to urge his horse on, then circled back as George continued on ahead.

“Young William,” he called, and Bill sprang to attention.

“Yes?”

“You take care of your family, and your horse. Keep your eyes open and your wits about you. Do that, you won’t never fail nobody, leastwise yourself.”

Bill nodded gravely.

“I will,” he said, and Horace gave a quick nod back, then urged Rogue to a trot.

The family went inside to clean up breakfast and prepare for the day, but Bill stayed where he was, watching Horace ride away, even after the horseman had disappeared into the landscape.

Bill remained on the grassy slope downhill from the new house. The girls were probably clearing the breakfast table and fixing the beds, and Pa would be getting ready to ride over to Doc Hathaway’s to help build his house. Pa had asked Bill to remain behind on the claim with Ma and the girls and take charge of things. The animals would need looking after, and there was still plenty of wood to be split for the new stable.

But for now Bill sat on the hillside, the new house at his back, taking in the sight of the countryside. The land had gone from being just another claim site to a real home that week. They were a Kansas family now, one of the first. Bill thought how different they seemed from the Codys who had left Iowa less than two months before. He felt years away from the little boy who had played Stagecoach Bill on a boulder back in LeClaire.

As he looked down over Salt Creek Valley, Bill could feel Sammy quietly beside him. It wasn't like the old ghost stories Joe Barnes used to tell. Rather, it was a sense of comfort, a just plain knowing. They were still together, in their way, and always would be.

He heard footsteps approaching through the grass behind him. He didn't even need to turn around—he knew it was Julia. He was surprised—and pleased, though he'd never admit it—that she'd sought him out. She sat down next to him, and neither spoke for several moments as the morning breeze blew over their heads.

"Iowa seems like a whole lifetime ago, don't you think?" Julia finally said.

Bill nodded. It's just the way he would have put it.

"I feel so different now, Bill," she continued, looking at her brother. "Like I'm a whole new person. Are the old Julia and Bill, the ones we were in LeClaire, are they gone, too?"

"No, they ain't," Bill replied. "Not by a long shot. You and me are the same as we ever were, but we're more now, too. Seen more, done more. Asked a little more of ourselves."

"Tried a little harder," Julia added, and Bill nodded.

"What were you thinking about just now, when I walked up?" Julia said after another pause.

"Sammy," he said.

Julia nodded. "So many times I've wished he'd come along with us. Wondered how things would feel if Sammy were here, too. Sometimes things still don't seem right with him gone. I guess we'll always miss him."

"In a way, yeah," said Bill. "But what I was kind of realizing just now is that he is here with us, only in a different way. That he crossed two states and a river just as sure as we did. There were times I was afraid that leaving LeClaire meant losing him altogether, but I see now that ain't so. You just got to know where to look, is all."

Julia didn't say anything, but she gazed around at the landscape with a contented expression.

"I think we're gonna be happy here, Julia," Bill said.

"I feel happy right now," she said. "What a lovely spot. Have you had a chance to do any exploring?"

"Not as much as I'd like," Bill replied. He turned around and looked toward the house for a moment. "Doesn't look like Pa's saddled up Little Gray yet. Could be time for a quick game of Lewis and Clark before he goes. What do you say?"

"Oh Bill," Julia said. "I don't know. I should be getting back to my chores—"

"Don't be silly," Bill interrupted. "We know we can't play games whenever we please, but that doesn't mean we have to stop forever. The girls are up safe at the house, and chores that been waiting all morning can wait a few minutes more."

Julia looked out over the ocean of grass and its inviting green waves.

"Do you really think there's time?" she asked.

Bill laughed. "All the time in the world. Time enough to start anything at all."

He stood up and pulled his sister to her feet.

Their journey had just begun.

AFTERWORD

★ ★ ★

Bill Cody's story is true. In 1854, when his family made their covered-wagon journey from Iowa to Kansas Territory, William Frederick Cody was still years away from the nickname that would stick with him as he became world famous: Buffalo Bill. What we know of the events surrounding the *adult* Bill's life as a frontiersman, scout, and Wild West showman is often a blend of fact with fiction, and it is difficult to tell where one leaves off and the other begins. The historical occurrences unfolding in this book as the Cody family moved to Kansas Territory are considerably better documented, however.

The framework of events experienced by Bill

and his family in this book is all true. Many of the people we meet along the way, including Joe Barnes, George Yancey, Mrs. Burns, Elijah Cody, and Horace Billings, are real. Turk, Little Gray, and Prince are all real animals. And Bill's ma and pa, five sisters, and brother, Sammy, are also all real people. I collected the known facts about these people and their lives from historians, biographers, and most importantly the two autobiographies written by Bill and his sister Julia. To fill in the rest, I relied on books, newspaper accounts, and diaries of people living in the same time and place as Bill and his family. I also crossed Iowa and Missouri and traveled into Kansas myself, though my rental car got me there considerably quicker than the thirty or so days it took the Codys in their covered wagon.

One other thing helped me identify with the Codys. I was born a Cody, too, so the name and history of the Cody family have always been of great importance to me. Like Buffalo Bill, my father was William Frederic Cody, though his middle name has no *k*. Dad was named after yet a third William Frederic Cody, a man whose Civil War rifle now hangs in my living room. Our Cody family lore always held that my father and Buffalo Bill were related by a common ancestor. I certainly grew up considering Buffalo Bill to be a kind of highly esteemed and famous cousin from way back.

My wonderful father is gone now, and so is my opportunity to ask what he thought the link between our families was. As I continue to write about young Bill and his family of Codys, I'll be looking for hints and clues that might shed some light on this little mystery. Bill's story is a long and fascinating one, and however it is looked at, one must agree that his life was never dull.